Daily Bread

RUSSELL MARTIN

DAILY BREAD

SAY YES QUICKLY BOOKS

Also by Russell Martin

Cowboy

Entering Space, with Joseph P. Allen

Matters Gray and White

The Color Orange

Beautiful Islands

A Story That Stands Like a Dam

Out of Silence

Beethoven's Hair

Picasso's War

The Sorrow of Archaeology

Say Yes Quickly Books

7715 East Highland Avenue

Scottsdale, Arizona 85251 USA

sayyesquickly.net

Ordering Information: Discounts for quantity sales are available for bookstores, corporations, associations, and others. For details, contact the "Special Sales Department" at the address above.

Library of Congress Control Number: 2021924567

Daily Bread / Russell Martin. -- 1st ed.

ISBN: 978-0-9965592-3-2

for Ian Martin Drummond,
Silas Martin Hatch,
Zane Russell Sternberg, and
Thomas Martin Nibley Nanson

The sky is the daily bread of the eyes.

RALPH WALDO EMERSON,
journal entry, May 25, 1843

THE OLD SHOWMAN seemed astonished by the size of the crowd—fifty thousand Denver citizens, maybe more, braving the frigid February weather to see this curious symbol of the new century attempt to climb into the sky. Dressed in high black boots and a fringed leather duster, his long white hair flowing from beneath his signature broad and loose-brimmed beaver hat, Bill Cody was arguably the city's most celebrated resident, surely its most stylish, and he made no attempt at anonymity that day. It made sense, after all, that storied Buffalo Bill would be on hand to see this aerial show of shows.

Organizers of the three-day exposition in Overland Park had secured a special viewing section for the city's social elite, but the crowd on the first afternoon was far larger than had been expected, and the single rope meant to separate men like Cody and my father—as well as my brother and me—from the larger and less-distinguished populace long since had been trampled, Cody laughing good-naturedly, I remember, as he was jostled by the press of people, wishing out loud that folks were this eager to see *his* show, suggesting that he might have to hire this fool aviator himself.

A wire fence separated those of us in the crowd from the flat dirt strip where the flying machine waited—a bi-winged airplane whose skin was yellow linen, simply a big box kite with a propeller attached, or so it appeared from some distance, the huge crowd careful not to crush the fence and get *too* close to the thing that surely would fall from the sky like a stone if it ever were airborne.

Yet just two weeks before, Frenchman Louis Paulhan—the papers called him "the Birdman"—had flown repeatedly in this same contraption at the Los Angeles Aviation Meet, making his subsequent appearance in Denver the cause of such keen anticipation. Paulhan's Farman biplane, shipped to Denver by boxcar, would leave the ground at 2:00 p.m. on February 1, 1910, the exposition's organizers had announced in thousands of handbills, then head south for sixty miles, where the Birdman would circle lofty Pike's Peak before his return to the city. The idea was outlandish, of course—even people who knew a bit about the nascent science of aviation remained uncertain whether an airplane *could* fly in Denver's insubstantial mile-high air, let alone at twice that altitude, but Paulhan intended to try, or so his promoters maintained.

My brother, whom everyone in the family called Young Roger— as tall as my father already but at least a hundred pounds lighter— craned his neck to see as at last the yellow box began to shudder and to move. Not quite fourteen, and two years Young Roger's junior, I was too short to see above the mass of heads and hats, but Bill Cody offered me the folding stool he'd brought along, and standing precariously on its leather seat, Cody's massive hands around my middle, I could watch as the machine slowly turned toward us, then aimed itself straight down the dirt track.

I could hear its motor throttle up, the propeller spinning so fast it seemed to disappear, and then I and all the citizens of Denver held our breaths because—who knew?—even breathing might disturb the enormous bird as it struggled to claim the sky. Yet there was no striving, no leaping upward like a cat trying to capture a moth. Unlike every bird that ever flew, this machine's wings did not flap, did not cup air and push it away like a swimmer carving a stroke. The Birdman throttled his engine hard, then somehow set it loose, the yellow box lumbering down the track, gaining speed, *racing* across the ground until, unbelievably, the box began to lift into the sky, fifty thousand folks gasping in unison, it seemed, then cheering wildly as Paulhan's airplane cleared the electric lines at the far end of the field, cleared the houses and the leaf-stripped tops of the trees, soaring steadily, gracefully, seeming to shrink as it sailed up and away, the wild crowd believing it now because *there it was* to see, yet it was visible only a minute more before the miraculous machine simply flew away.

How long would it take the Birdman to reach Pike's Peak? Would he freeze to death if he climbed high enough to circle the mountain? When would this heroic man return to Denver and to earth? There were no immediate answers to the flood of questions that suddenly begged to be asked, but because the sight had seemed so impossible, so utterly unreal, half of the fifty thousand surely also asked the single question for which their fellows could offer a firm reply: Did you see? Did you see the Birdman fly away in his yellow box? Could you see it, Son?, Bill Cody asked in my direction.

I saw, I told him. You think he's coming back?

He'll have to if he wants to repeat the stunt tomorrow, my father said.

I wish Mum had come, Young Roger said. But she and Louisa Cody had met for tea instead of joining the mass descension on Overland Park, the two women announcing that they didn't have the stomachs for watching a man die in a fall from the sky.

Tell her she's a fool for missing it, Father said to Young Roger. Tell her she's a silly woman.

I'll bring her with me tomorrow, I offered brightly.

You won't miss school a second day, he assured me instead.

But . . . she *has* to see it, doesn't she? It's near a miracle, and she'd best see it with her own eyes.

There are plenty of miracles that women pay no heed to. Isn't that so, Bill?

Oh, I'm old enough, smart enough, never to discuss the subject of women, Cody said, his eyes twinkling. They're as mysterious, and *wonderful*, let's say, as that flying machine. Do you suppose I could get him to travel with the show?

Yes, and me and Young Roger along as his assistants, I pleaded.

Absolutely, Young Roger agreed.

Fine, then, said the showman, his white Vandyke framing his broad and beneficent smile. We'll link the last century with the new one, from open wilderness to machines that ride on the wind. But he won't come cheap, that's a certainty. I may have to go hat in hand to see my banker. Cody angled this comment at my father.

Your banker, as it happens, could probably be talked into financing such foolishness, my father told him. Although I can't imagine how these airplanes will ever amount to anything, the masses seem willing to squander their pennies to see them.

I'd pay all I had to go up in one, I vowed.

Oh, you would, would— Father stopped as a sudden rumor rushed through the animated crowd: He's coming back! See! The yellow dot. It's the Birdman, back already!

No one could be certain whether Louis Paulhan had flown to Pike's Peak in the half hour since he had disappeared. There hardly seemed to have been time, yet who knew how fast his machine could soar? Perhaps airplanes gained enormous speed as they climbed into the rarefied mountain air. But what *was* a bright yellow certainty now was the Birdman's triumphant return. His big box kite was heading home, aimed as directly, it seemed, at the mass of fifty thousand as at the flat dirt track beside them. People at the far end of the field even began to try to escape their proximity to the field, afraid that the airplane was intent on them, before at last it was clear that everyone was safe and that the machine would touch down right where it had left the ground, its rubber tires kicking up a quick cloud of dust as they skidded and bounced and then began to roll, the roar from the crowd tumultuous now, Louis Paulhan pulling himself from the cockpit and standing up high to wave, my brother and I dumbstruck with excitement yet buoyant, too, with delight, Bill Cody leaning into our father's ear to shout that yes, there was much to talk about.

IT HAD BEEN the most stupendous sight I'd ever seen, and I ached to think that my mother had missed it, that I might not see it once more tomorrow or the next day or ever again in my life. During dinner that evening, I had been unable to convince my mother to join Young Roger and me to go see the Birdman fly the following day, and neither had I made headway with either parent and my carefully articulated argument that the importance of school paled in comparison with the magic of the modern age. Mother simply was too afraid of what *might* go wrong with the Birdman's flying apparatus, she said. The danger surely was far too great. And she chose not to offer a counterpoint to Father's commandment, expressed again as we sat at the long dining table, that both Young Roger and I would be at Grayland School as usual on the next two afternoons, and nowhere near the yellow machine that waited near the river in lowland Overland Park.

Yet although Young Roger was grudgingly willing to acquiesce to our parents' demands, I simply could not. Ordinarily, I would have obeyed them without much bother, but in this instance they surely were mistaken about what mattered for a fellow's education, so I simply stole away from school at one o'clock on the following afternoon and negotiated the tramway routes that took me to the park. The crowd seemed every bit as big again that day, bigger even, and although the reserved section was better secured this time, I knew I wouldn't be admitted there alone, so I followed a group of boys who had crawled under a sheep-wire fence and had found their own privileged viewing position on the roof of an aging bandstand.

What a spot it was from which to watch the Birdman, a scarlet scarf draped round his neck today, the strap of his leather helmet left unclasped. One of the boys, a wiry little fellow with a thick thatch of curly hair whom his friends called Avi, evidently had seen the flight the day before, but the rest of the pack had not, and as Paulhan pressed himself into the cockpit and began to maneuver the airplane into position, Avi offered an animated account of what we were about to see. And for a second day, the yellow kite sped down the track, again it soared into the sky and a second time it disappeared. As it had the day before, the huge crowd exploded with wonder and delight, and the knot of boys—with me mated to them now—screamed and jumped and nearly brought the bandstand down in our excitement as the Birdman's miracle unfolded and the airplane flew away, but then Avi bore the sobering news that the craft would not draw near Pike's Peak in the minutes of its absence. They say he turned around right about Sedalia yesterday, Avi announced. Anyway, the airplane would break to bits if he tried to fly as high as the mountain. They say the air has ice up there that would rip it to bitty shreds.

This fellow Avi seemed to be a fountain of information, and I was glad to have encountered him, happy as well as to have joined him and his pals on their perfect perch. I wondered how Avi could know so much about air and aviation, and I paid attention when—just as the Birdman reappeared in the southern sky—Avi announced that one day he would have an airplane himself and become Colorado's own aviator hero. But before I could ask how he planned to set his fine future in motion, Avi had bounded down from the bandstand, the other boys in his pursuit, and they were racing toward the end of the field where Paulhan was about to bring his flying box to a triumphant rest. I longed to follow them again, to see the flying machine up close and maybe see the set of the Birdman's eyes, but I *had* to get home, I knew, and I climbed down—thrilled and downcast in the same instant—pushing my way through thousands of sunny people who were enchanted by what they'd seen. And as I stood on the running board of an overflowing streetcar headed toward home, my face pressed into the head wind it engendered, I imagined myself as an intrepid aviator as well one day.

My brother wasn't home yet, I discovered when I burst into the house; my mother was attending a card party, my father was still at work at the bank on Seventeenth Street, and my secret was safe. But how could I keep it quiet? How could I resist telling them I'd seen the Birdman soar a *second* time and that I'd met a friendly boy bent on being an aviator too? Outside again, I crawled under the back hedge and into Cheesman Park, running now for little reason other than to spill my manic energy, my arms spread wide on the chance that they would lift me off the ground. Buoyant, euphoric, my running a little like flying, I was sure, I raced to the park's edge at Thirteenth Avenue, a horse in harness shying from me as it passed, the buggy's driver shouting something I couldn't hear. But then I did hear a sound I recognized—the churn and rasp and throaty gurgle of my father's Maxwell cabriolet, heading south down Humboldt Street toward home at a strangely early hour. He must have gone to see the Birdman again, I decided as I raced toward the sound—that had to explain why my father was early today—and as I saw the motorcar make its way toward me, I *knew* I could share my secret and I waved in celebration, catching Father's eye, eliciting from him something akin to a smile, stepping out of the Maxwell's path, then ably leaping onto its running board and grabbing hold, my father neither welcoming me aboard nor scowling at the stunt, shouting *hello* at him, shouting *I saw it, too,* in the second before my father swung the motorcar into the drive and I lost my grip in the sweep of the sudden turn, tumbling into the street, a back tire barely missing me as my father braked to a panicked stop and rushed around the rear of the Maxwell to the spot where I lay motionless, bleeding and unconscious from the impact of my head against the curb.

ALTHOUGH MY HEAD was pounding and everything I saw from the bed was bent and blurry, I recognized my room, my mother close beside me, and there stood Anne-Marie, our family's cook, when at last I stirred at half past six or so. Her face radiant and wet with tears, my mother kissed my cheek and whispered, Good evening, my little man, as she saw me come to life, and I tried to say hello in response but the word stuck in my mouth. Anne-Marie had brought me warm consommé in a cup, but neither could I drink, and my mother caressed my forehead with her delicate fingers and told me not to worry; I would be fine, and only rest was what I needed now.

In the sitting room downstairs, my father and Dr. Galen Locke sat smoking, and the news from Anne-Marie that I had roused was cause as well for brandy. Although I had been unconscious when Locke first examined me, I learned later from my mother that the doctor had been quick to assure his friends that the cut on their son's head was minor, that he would come round and be well as soon as his brain had some time to settle. The brain is a gelatinous substance, Dr. Locke had explained, and a blow like the one the boy took sets it quivering wildly. But as long as the skull isn't fractured, then it's quite safe and cannot be seriously injured.

Just as the doctor had said it would, my brain had stopped trembling by morning and my headache had disappeared, and although I did not see the Birdman fly high into the sky a third miraculous time, my mother's efforts to confine me to my bed failed entirely on the second morning after the accident. I arrived at the breakfast table as if the injury were old news, ready for school but willing—if that was what they thought was best—to stay home another day at my parents' insistence. But it seemed to my father that I was well enough, at least, to be scolded for my stunt, and he informed me that I would spend afternoons in my bedroom for a month, as well as clean the coal bin, if I *ever* did anything similarly idiotic again. When I realized that leaping onto the motorcar was the only crime for which I had to answer—that my father hadn't heard my shouted news of my return to Overland Park, and that my secret still was safe—I was quickly contrite and I assured them that I had learned an important lesson. Young Roger, also ignorant of my secret expedition, nonetheless could sense that my remorse was a trifle over the top, and he advised me that I'd best buy some work gloves because I'd be in the coal bin before the week was out.

For the moment, at least, I avoided further punishment from my father, but two days later my mother bore the brunt of his ready anger when she told him the accident had been his fault as much as mine. What had he been *thinking* when he let me ride the last block home? Our parents had adjourned from the dinner table and had gone up to their suite for the Sunday afternoon respite they called their private time when we heard the shouting begin. It reached a crescendo with the slamming of a bedroom door and our father's loud descent down the stairs and departure from the house, the Maxwell's engine cranking moments later, the house soon quiet again and the two of us returning to the checkerboard that occupied the rest of that snowy February afternoon, our mother coming down at last at six to join us for a bit of supper, the left half of her face red and swollen, an eye already darkening, neither of us daring to inquire whether she was all right because this was a circumstance that our family played out with regularity, Young Roger and I apprehending that our only role was to pretend not to notice anything awry, our mother in turn always rebounding with a kind of lighthearted, if nonetheless injured, ease.

It was the next time my father's temper exploded, the next time my mother felt the sting of his words and his hand, when I was felled by my first spell. The winter night was hushed and frozen two weeks later when Father responded with theatrical outrage as my mother noted that she'd surely need to reset the buttons of his waistcoats if he grew much broader. Although we had seen through the years the regular evidence our mother wore of slaps and punches, neither of us actually had ever seen our father strike her until that night. As my father's curse swelled into a scream and a sudden blow landed against my mother's head, she shrank back protectively against the loveseat where she'd been sitting. Lying on the Persian carpet that framed the sitting area, I suddenly lunged at my father's feet. Flying at him without thinking except—instinctively—to separate him from my mother, I clung to his trousers and tried to tackle him, but instead he spun and seized me by the belt and tossed me aside in a single motion, sending me skidding off the carpet and onto the hardwood floor. I struggled to my feet as my father stormed out of the room, but then collapsed, convulsing, my four limbs flailing wildly, as my mother later described it, my eyes turned back their sockets, my breaths a staccato spasm, my urine pooling on the polished floor.

Reaching me in an instant, terrified, I'm sure, by what in the world was besetting me, Mother tried to quiet me, tried to still my wild movements, but she could not calm me, my arms flailing at her as she attempted to smother the convulsions, my blanched face consumed by what she said was a horrifying kind of absence, Mother shouting to Young Roger to telephone for an ambulance, *quickly!,* my father reappearing in the room as enraged as when he'd left it, offering no assistance and apparently unconcerned, simply marching past the place on the floor where I and my mother lay, her skirts soaked with my pee and her terror total now because I was still in the grip of a thing she couldn't conceive of as my father slammed the foyer door behind him and disappeared into the frigid February night.

THE PHYSICIAN WHO attended to me at St. Luke's Hospital had told my mother—no doubt still beside herself with worry despite the fact that my convulsions at last had ceased—that her son had suffered what he called an epileptic seizure. But two days later, when Dr. Locke returned at my father's request to the house on Humboldt Street to look me over again, he scoffed at the diagnosis.

These young bucks are so quick to spot disease these days, he loudly announced to my parents as they stood in the hallway outside my bedroom. They don't believe they're doing their business unless they pounce on something sinister. Epilepsy, in point of fact, is a congenital disorder, and if this were epilepsy, surely we'd have seen it emerge before age—what did you say?—thirteen? Dr. Locke's diagnosis, on the other hand, had a simpler but rather more delicate explanation, one that had to do with vapors and exuberant energy and the emergence into manhood, and he had asked to speak with my father privately to discuss it in more detail.

For my part, I felt fit and healthy enough again. I had a fresh scar on my forehead, but it would fade, and all I could make of the spell was that it had come and gone and evidently had left me no worse for wear. Yet it did seem odd to me when my father insisted that the two of us walk in Cheesman Park one evening late in the month as a hint of spring blew into the city on a southern breeze.

As we walked the oval pathway, my father was full of unusual talk about procreation and what he called the male's place in the mystery, informing me that healthy living demanded that seeds be sown solely where they were intended, then changing the subject, or so it seemed, to say that it was time I joined him and Young Roger for boxing at Becker's Gymnasium on Saturdays. There's nothing that beats the pugilistic arts, my father maintained, for the channeling of excess energy. He said, too, that he planned to hang a punching bag in the basement, one he and we could use as often as we liked, and I wished I could tell him that yes, it was surely a fine idea for *him* to have something new in the house to hit.

Although boxing didn't hold real appeal for me—especially on those weekend mornings when my father insisted that Young Roger and I spar headlong with each other, the result always that I was beaten and bleeding from the nose by the time my father whistled the fight to a merciful finish—I was game at least, taking punches to the belly and the head without a whimper, sometimes even landing a blow to my brother's jaw that would win my father's nod of approval, Father declaring, Yes, damnit, you're a fighter!, as I flailed away.

But when I had a second spell in March while battling inside the ring, he seemed at once incensed by its onset and unconcerned about my welfare, leaving me unattended as I thrashed and contorted and at last lay splayed on the canvas. I'm not going to have this!, he shouted as I finally lifted myself to an elbow. I won't have you abusing yourself and inciting this business! Your brother doesn't stoop to such filthy stuff, my father scolded, but I didn't know what the stuff was to which he referred, and neither did Young Roger seem to know when I asked him as our father showered.

Just the fits, I guess, Young Roger told me. I guess he thinks you don't have to have them.

Both times, I said, I could feel something peculiar, only for a second, before I blacked out. But I couldn't stop it, because it seemed like it just had to start.

I suffered another spell in Becker's boxing ring before my father announced that I didn't deserve to learn to fight if I was intent on reducing myself to the animal level. You're no better than a stud dog licking his private parts, he snarled, driving away soon thereafter in the Maxwell with only Young Roger in his company, Father suggesting to him that they enjoy a Saturday luncheon at the Brown Palace Hotel, leaving me, woozy and weak and still unsteady on my feet, to find my own way home.

My arrival home alone in the middle of the afternoon—my haggard countenance and the confession that I'd had another fit, which my father hadn't stomached—was enough to spark a new confrontation between Mother and my father when the two Rogers returned, Father leaving in the house in the noisy huff that was his habit when she implored him to consider the possibility that I was injured, asking him to consider why women suffered spells as well if Dr. Locke's theory was right, Father solely contending in response that he wouldn't claim a son who was a weakling or a sissy-boy or a pervert, pushing her away in a fury, sending her tumbling against an armoire when she clutched his lapels and begged him to stay and talk this out with her, Father hissing, It's him or me in this bloody house, before he flew out of the bedroom and she collapsed on their bed and tried to be quiet as she cried, although I'd heard it all.

TWO SPELLS IN day-short April, three more in the month of May, then I was felled by another fit on the fifth of June, my brother's sixteenth birthday, the garden crowded with guests, a brass band entertaining them from the gazebo, my father tapping his glass with a dinner knife to draw people's attention, ready to toast his namesake and eldest son just as I fell to the grass. I know that every muscle in my body must have seized, then trembled wildly; I vomited that time, and a friend of my mother who apparently had some experience in these circumstances scooped the stuff out of my mouth before it blocked my breathing. Urine stained my new white trousers, and I'm sure I must have lain on the lawn in a ghastly way that seemed to my father to ridicule our entire family, mocking him most particularly, all he had striven for, everything he ever had provided.

Young Roger told me that I was still convulsing when three waiters carried me inside, followed by Dr. Locke, who evidently made a great show of his willingness to be of service as he departed the garden. And I suppose my father did his best to revive the festivities, gathering the guests' attention again as soon as I was out of sight, assuring them of the certainty that his youngest son would be all right, thanking Dr. Locke, who was absent, then asking Young Roger to come stand beside him, reminding everyone of the reason for their celebration.

His charity had escaped him, however, by the time Father had said farewell to the last of the guests at dusk and climbed the stairway to the second floor where he found Mother seated on my bed, pressing a cold cloth to my forehead. Leave the little bugger alone!, he demanded as he marched into the room. He doesn't deserve one moment of your attention. The boy deserves neither you nor me nor the home we have provided him. These fits are his foul handiwork and I've had the last of them! It's him or me in this house. Have your pick.

Dear, please, she implored him, going to him, taking his arm. He has a horrible headache still, and I *swear* to you that these aren't his fault. *Please.*

I've never been more embarrassed in my life, he fumed.

It doesn't matter. No one thought the—

It doesn't *matter*? Father was infuriated now. You stupid creature, it matters in every way imaginable! I have a name to protect, a reputation to sustain, and that little shithole does this to me?

He shares your name, she reminded him in the instant before he slapped her, his open hand striking her face hard, sending her reeling to the bed where I was struggling to rise, attempting to stand and defend my mother, lunging at my father before I, too, was hit, my father's hand folded into a fist this time, his fat knuckles finding my jaw and dropping me to the floor like a bantam fighter felled by a heavyweight, Father beating me in retribution for embarrassment, beating me because these fits now seemed to fill our days.

IF IT CAME down to me or my father, then I simply would steal away, I decided. I could make a go of it on my own; I was thirteen and a half, almost—and I was clever and could work. I had clothes enough, and there was a little money from my grandparents Hegarty that I had put away. I wasn't certain yet where I would live; maybe I'd be a vagabond, or perhaps I could work for Bill Cody and travel the world with his show; *maybe* I'd follow the Birdman from town to town. I didn't like to imagine my mother without me, the two Rogers her only household companions, but I would talk to my brother and make him swear that he'd defend her forever from our father's blows.

On the Sunday morning after the birthday party and my very public *faux paus*, I told my mother my head still hurt too much for me to go to church, and while my parents and my brother were attending the ten o'clock communion service at the Church of the Ascension—my Catholic parents had become Episcopalians when they married because they would meet and mix with better people, my father had insisted—I packed clothes and shoes, an overcoat, even galoshes and mittens despite the summer weather, my money, and the *Book of Common Prayer* my parents had given me at my confirmation into a tattered suitcase I found in the basement. I brushed my teeth and donned clean clothes and wore my favorite shoes; and I wrote a note that explained my departure, leaving it on my bed: *I am sorry about these fits. I don't know why I'm having them, but I wish I wasn't. Until they are over, I'd best leave you all some peace. I'll be fine, and I'll be in touch when I can. (Young Roger, you can use anything in here that you like.) Your Son, Thomas Dumont.*

Then I headed downtown, intending to walk to save my money, but boarding a streetcar on Colfax Avenue when my case grew too heavy, cognizant of who and what I was leaving but uncertain about my destination, unconcerned about it, in fact, until the moment when I first considered where I would sleep that night. I could get a bed in a rooming house, I realized, but I wasn't sure how much it would cost, and whatever the price, I'd probably better protect my funds, I decided, until I'd found some way to replenish them. And the weather was warm anyway; why not camp down on the river, maybe meet some bindle men, maybe learn how to hop the rails and wander far afield. But then again, perhaps it was a better plan to stay in Denver for a while, a place where I knew the territory and how to get around. I'd fend for myself for the summer, then surely Bill Cody would hire me on in the autumn and I could begin to travel far afield.

I stepped down from the tramway at Curtis Street—a wondrous stretch of blocks I knew well and normally delighted in, its rows of cinemas and theaters familiar to me from dozens of Saturday afternoons spent deep in their welcoming darkness, transfixed by the exotic images that danced on their screens and moved across their stages, their marquees and high facades lit with a million electric lights, or so people said, enough at least to dazzle Thomas

Edison when he had come to town. Yet Curtis Street was all but deserted on that Sunday morning, the bright lights darkened and only world-weary sweepers and window-washers out on the littered sidewalks. I read the movie posters for a while—and I reckoned I might even spend a dime to see *Indian Massacre* some rainy day—then I wandered over to Market Street, where I asked a saloonkeeper in an apron who was leaning in the open doorway of his establishment if he had any work a fellow might do for pay.

Not on a Sunday morning with God and the governor watching, I don't, the bartender told him. You old enough to work, are you?

I'm seventeen tomorrow. I'm just a little short, is all, but I'm a good worker.

Where you traveling from? The man pointed to my suitcase.

Well . . . Kansas mostly. The prairies of Kansas, Sir. Would you know of an inexpensive place where I could board?

You mean cheap or are you looking for free of charge?

Well, Sir, free would be fine for now, I'd say.

Then pick out a doorway, Son. But leave your case in a locker at Union Station or some thief will separate it from you. Spend your pennies on a locker, and you can wash at the station too, then sleep anywhere you like. And come back here when I'm open and I'll buy you your first Denver beer.

I thanked the fellow for his suggestions, and said sure, I'd be back, you bet I would. And although I never returned, it was the saloon man's sage advice that set me on my way. Union Station proved to be the perfect headquarters for a fellow starting out on his own. I could rent a locker for a nickel a day; the toilets were clean and as big as ballrooms and the shoeshines who inhabited them didn't seem to mind frequent visitors, especially if you had them polish your shoes once in every while. The great hall was filled with row after row of high-backed benches that looked like enormous pews, and although the men who worked for the stationmaster would roust you if they found you, they didn't go on regular patrol and a bench made a fine sort of bed.

The summer nights were cool and the rush and gurgle of the water made camping at the river's edge a pleasure—lots of fellows gathering there, men of all ages and races, most of whom had been born someplace far away and had come to Denver seeking something better. There'd be a bonfire everywhere a group of four or five were camped, and the fire always attracted three or four more solitary fellows like me. Many of them were bindle men who made a habit of sojourning in Denver in the summertime; others were established residents—some for many years—who simply lacked the means to find more formal housing; a few were boys as young as I was, although they appeared to come from very different sorts of families. One boy I liked said he didn't believe he ever had a ma or pa; another fellow's father had been a miner, killed in an explosion, his mother now working the line—as he described her occupation—up in Central City, although he said he hadn't seen her in a couple of years and couldn't be sure where she was spreading her legs these days.

I was one of the few fellows at the river, young or old, who could read and write, and although my skills never made me money, they did garner me a small measure of esteem. Someone would find a discarded newspaper and insist that I read it aloud by the firelight— one foul-smelling fellow who never traveled anywhere, as far as I could tell, always determined to hear the departure schedules of the trains; a man missing a leg below one knee taking curious pleasure in hearing the obituaries, saying aloud that he liked the thought that the fancy people also had to die. On occasion, someone would find or even buy a dime novel, and on those nights at the edge of the Platte, I would seem to some of them to be capable of a kind of magic, reading aloud a tale of high adventure and intrigue, transfixing the fellows with the words I spoke, sometimes begging for sleep when I grew tired and bleary eyed, but always forced to finish the riveting story I had started.

What my comrades offered me in return was their survivors' wisdom, what they'd learned along the way that made the alley life a little easier: how the delivery men returning to the Beatrice Creamery in the afternoons would give away milk that had got too warm; how sometimes, too, you could get good day-work chopping ice at the creamery when the weather was stifling hot; the fact that Morey Mercantile sold thick packing blankets for a buck; the point of view that hat and coat racks and their contents could be considered public property; the way to bust inside a warehouse loading-door when the weather was cold and killing; how a fellow could get drunk on a nickel a day, and smoke for free, and find a girl for fifty cents if she didn't have to be pretty, although I hadn't yet been brave enough to try. Most of all, the men who slept in doorways, under the bridges that spanned the creek, and at the grassy riverside taught me a kind of confident resourcefulness, the sense that all a fellow had to do was put his mind to his immediate predicament, to his daily desires and his needs, the certainty that the only essential difference between one man and another was how fat or slim his wallet was.

My persistent spells did not abate once I was on my own, but neither did they grow more constant. Three weeks, even an entire month might pass before a fit would follow the one that preceded it, but two spells might come back to back during the worst of weeks. Although I still couldn't fathom their cause—except to be sure somehow that Dr. Locke's notion of vapors and energy and insistent desire could not account for them—I had grown able by now to sense when a fit was on its way. My mouth would begin to taste odd, as if were filled with metal, as though I'd been sucking on nickels like they were sunflower seeds. Sometimes, suddenly, my eyes would go haywire and the light would flicker and pulse and dance; rarely, strangely, I'd have the fleeting sense that I was bound to heaven in an airplane, clouds parting to allow my passage and angels waving their welcomes in the instant before the image vanished and the spell commenced.

Always, a spell would leave me utterly spent, my head throbbing unmercifully for hours, for days, my tongue bitten and bleeding oftentimes, my energy entirely drained; and many times it seemed to me that I no longer could think. In the dull and dreary aftermath of a fit, I would lie on my blankets beside the Platte and do no more than listen to the passing water, too groggy to read or talk. When the weather was wet or cold, when an early snow settled on the bustling city, I would find what shelter I could—the basement boiler rooms of hotels, warm and hospitably dark; the grain bins at the breweries, where heaps of hops and barley made agreeable beds; the hard and high-backed benches at the train depot always were an option, and occasionally I would even land in a bona fide bed that smelled of sweat and perfume when the matron at a women's hotel where I was scrubbing floors and cleaning toilets would recognize that I was ill and insist that I stop and sleep.

I often remembered my mother, and I was aware of how much I missed her when someone like Tessa Randolph, whom the fellows called Big Tess, would demand that I strip out of my hideous clothes and bathe in the brass tub on the third floor of her brothel, then tuck me between browning sheets on the bed in the little room that was adjacent to her own, telling me my work could wait until I felt some better. I had written my mother twice in the half-year since I'd walked away from home, knowing she always was the first to see the mail and assuring her that I was fine and that my spells hadn't worsened. And although I wasn't certain I should have, I told her, too, that I was still in Denver—not a runaway but just a fellow who'd left home sooner than some boys did—and I wanted her to know that one day when I was sure she'd be alone, I'd venture out to see her.

I knew my parents had tried hard for a while to find me. I'd seen flyers pasted to lampposts, in fact, and an old fellow named Harry with whom I often wiled away evenings down at the river liked to joke that if he ever were desperate for five dollars, he would tuck me under his arm and haul me home to my nursemaid and my mansion, unfolding the tattered flyer he kept in his coat as proof that he knew one or two of my secrets. Once, a cop who had caught me coming out of a window on Wazee Street demanded to know my name and where I lived, and although a name had come to me readily enough, I stammered awkwardly about my residence, and the stony cop inquired, You ain't that runaway rich kid, are you?

No, I told him. But I know who you mean, and I saw that kid.

He's taller than me by a head and his hair is black as coal. He was poking through the bins in the alley behind the Windsor not an hour ago. I bet he's still there. Surely the cop imagined winning a handsome finder's fee if he were the one who returned the fancy man's son, and his interest in me therefore ended abruptly, the cop simply telling me to stay out of places I didn't belong before he marched off to snare the runaway and the extra pay.

There were times, of course, when I was tempted simply to escort myself back to the house on Humboldt Street, to reclaim my room, my books, my collection of postcards painted with scenes of faraway places, my place at the dinner table. But it was that specific memory that always soured me on the prospect of going home—the four of us at the formal table every evening, my father seldom speaking and his silence always forbidding, his barbs aimed foremost at my mother until the fits commenced, when I became the central object of his wrath. When I pressed myself on sleepless nights to be honest about where I most would like to be, I always could reassure myself that, by damn, Denver, Colorado at large was home enough for now.

A KID COULD earn a dollar mucking out a saloon or rooming house; you could sell copies of the lurid *Post* on days when the red-ink headline shouted the birth of a two-headed calf, but only if first you had the means to buy yourself a stack. Yet once the weather turned, I discovered that my most dependable and even lucrative occupation was collecting sherds of coal along the railroad tracks that paralleled the river, then selling a bucket or two of warmth to the destitute Italians who lived in the Bottoms or to the recent immigrants in fat fur hats who walked the streets in Jew Town. It hadn't been my own entrepreneurial scheme—I'd heard about it from a fellow who swore the coal was there for the taking and that people were quick to pay when they were freezing—but it was work that seemed tailor-made for me. I could scavenge for coal even when I remained groggy in the aftermath of a fit; and when I was well it always felt fine to hike for miles along the tracks, the creosote that coated the ties smelling at once acrid and fragrant, the shiny rails warm in the winter sun, the tracks receding into the distance in a way that hinted at other worlds.

And it wasn't necessarily solitary work. On frigid days that promised brisk business, days when fresh snow had not buried the black nuggets we prized, half a dozen fellows—mostly youngsters who could bear the bending over—would be hoofing the tracks in the heart of the valley. There was coal enough for all of us, and when I was clear-headed I always was glad for the companionship and conversation. And I was amazed to find one morning in February to encounter the boy I had followed to the roof of the bandstand a year before to watch the Birdman fly.

Yep, I was there. Saw him all three days, the young man boasted. He was no taller than me; his knotted hair spilled out of a woolen cap, and his dark eyes seemed to sparkle with the memories of those stupendous days. My pals and me, we saw it all, and then I shook his hand, and sorely wished I spoke the French language. I would have liked to tell him I'd be following in his shoes.

You said the same the day I watched with you.

It's a fact.

I'd say the fact is that you're out with me collecting coal. I grinned at him, then thrust out my hand. Tommy Dumont is who I am.

Well, I'm Avram Sokolow. Avi is what they call me, and you're a son of a bitch, I'd say. The boy returned something of a smile but he was clearly piqued by the implication that he had a distance to go before he saw success. I may not have it all in hand quite today, but I'll get there. Christ, my name even sounds like *aviation*. I'll fly before you're done scrounging for this stuff, that's a bet.

I didn't mean disrespect, I told him. I hope you make it. I'd love to myself, truth to tell. Looks to me like the finest thing in the world, though I suppose you're actually out of the world once you're up in an airplane, aren't you?

Avi paused for a moment and seemed to enjoy the thought. I like that. The world is this hard thing here and when you soar in the sky you aren't in the world any more. That must be the way it is. Hey, you're not so bad. Tommy, did you say?

Yep. What I can't figure out is, if you're just a coal hound like me, how'd you get so smart about aviation? I remember you knew all about how the Frenchie was flying that day.

Well, I read the papers for one thing. Maybe you ought to learn how to read.

I can read, I said in response to what seemed to be Avi's turn at an insult.

Fair enough. That's one way. I read every word in every paper the days the Birdman was in town. Plus, I know a rich fellow from Capitol Hill. Ira Humphreys. They call him Bumps. Sometimes he's got a little work for me at his machine shop. He's crazy for motorcars and airplanes and anything with engines and moving parts. They say he's quite the whiz too. It was him who had the big hand in bringing the Birdman to town. Well, his old man's dough played a part. And Bumps Humphreys let me come look at the Birdman's machine along with a bunch of high-rollers on the third day. Louis Paulhan himself was there, just before he flew, and he talked about flying and showed us around, and a lady from the library, I think it was, translated what he said. That's when I shook his hand with this hand right here.

I glanced at Avi's right hand, as though it might look quite remarkable even a year after the encounter. I'm jealous of you, I told him. I saw the Birdman the first two days, but then I had a fall from my father's Maxwell and got banged up a bit and couldn't go back again.

You've got a father with a Maxwell? And you're out here mining coal? I don't get it. And how'd you fall out of it, for Christ's sake?

I was riding on the running board, and he turned a corner, and I guess I slipped. The rest is kind of complicated.

I'd take either a father or a Maxwell, Avi said. Either one sounds fine to me.

You don't have an old man?

Did. He's dead. Mother, too. We come here from New York when people said dry air and altitude was good for the consumption. They both had it bad, but mainly only spoke Russian, and neither of them ever found good work in goddamn Denver, so they just got sicker till they died. Four years ago. Mother on a Tuesday, my Pa gone by Saturday.

Son of a gun, I said, not knowing what else to say in the seconds before Avi stopped abruptly, stretching an arm out to halt me too, motioning with his head toward four men who seemed to have come out of nowhere and who now faced us from fifty yards down the track.

I hope you can run as well as read, Avi whispered. It's the cops and the railroad dicks. Wanting their coal back, the sons of bitches.

You sure? Nobody's ever bothered me about it before.

Then you're new at this game, aren't you? I don't know about you, but I'm not giving up a near-full bucket to the bastards. Come on!

Avi scrambled down a graveled slope that dropped sharply away from the railroad bed, then disappeared into a stand of willows with me close behind him, the willows' dormant branches bright red and easy enough to race through, my battered bucket still in tow. But the high, wire fence that marked the western perimeter of the stockyards soon blocked our progress, and we turned north and continued alongside it, Avi sure he had eluded capture until suddenly the willows disappeared and a meager road dead-ended at a stockyard gate and a Denver policeman rushed toward us wielding his billy-club.

That's far enough, you little louts!, shouted the cop. Stop right there.

Three other men, winded but only a few yards behind the policeman, soon surveyed us, and a gruff fellow with an ugly scar on his cheek readily recognized Avi.

You again, huh? I thought I'd warned you well against stealing railroad property, you little Jew-shit.

Must have been some other kid, Avi said breathlessly.

It was you, Kike boy. I recognize your oily fucking face. And this time I've got the law with me, and you and your fucking pal here are going to pay.

So, you want to make a complaint?, a second cop asked the man who recognized Avi.

We sure as holy hell do. I don't care what it is, they're stealing D&RG property.

It's just coal scrap, sir, I tried to explain. It just falls from the trains. We can make a few pennies selling it and an old lady stays warm that way.

We don't give a fuck about your old ladies, said another man who wore a beard and surely also worked for the railroad. If we let you punks come on the tracks and scavenge all winter, one of you'll get sliced in half by a train one day and then the papers'll scream that it's our fault.

Leave your buckets and let's go, the policeman said. You boys can tell your sob stories to the judge. Come on. *Now!*

Avi glared at the men who had him cornered, then flung the pebbled contents of his bucket at their feet. Mighty big stuff, ain't you? he challenged. You can go home and tell the missus tonight that you caught some real desperados. She might even let you have a little if I didn't wear her out too much this morning.

The man with the scar lunged at Avi, eager to take him on now, but the others held him back, and I stepped in front of my new friend, saying, So, let's go meet this judge and be done with it. But I believe I'll take my bucket with me so he can see the awful evidence.

JUDGE BEN LINDSEY had worked determinedly to establish a justice system tailored to the special circumstances of children in the first years of the new century, relentlessly lobbying the Colorado legislature in 1903 and again in 1907 for passage of what became known as the Lindsey law, requiring all children to attend school until age sixteen, creating a separate court for minors, one in which names were kept confidential and sentences were aimed at reform, and applying harsh penalties to adults who contributed to a child's dereliction. When I tracked it down a year or so ago in an ancient and musty and much-neglected edition of the Colorado Revised Statutes, it seemed curious to me that although Lindsey's law required that any delinquent child *shall be treated, not as a criminal, but as misdirected and misguided and needing aid and encouragement*, it also spelled out the myriad ways in which a child could go wrong, mandating the prosecution of anyone sixteen or under *who violates the laws of this state or is incorrigible; or who knowingly associates with thieves or immoral persons; or who is growing up in idleness or crime; or who visits a house of ill-repute; or who patronizes any saloon or dram shop or place where any gambling device is operated; or who patronizes any pool room or bucket shop; or who loiters about the street in the night; or who wanders about any railroad yard or tracks or who hooks onto any moving train; or who uses vile, obscene, vulgar, profane, or indecent language.*

Collecting the bits of coal that fell from the hoppers of passing trains, as it turned out, was illegal on several counts if you were still a boy, and although Avi Sokolow had been aware of the risks and possible punishment the occupation entailed, I certainly had not. You mean they can send a fellow to jail for scrounging *coal?* I asked him as we waited on a bench in a courthouse hallway, the railroad detectives departed by now but one of the stern policemen still standing by our side.

Not real jail, but there's a kids' jail off in Golden where they send the toughs. I was there for a while once. Mostly, though, they just tell you it's school or a job and take your pick. Act like you're sorry as all hell about what you did, and you'll be fine, Avi whispered.

But I *wasn't* contrite. I couldn't fathom why it was a crime for a fellow to walk the tracks, nor did I comprehend why a poor man who wanted the warmth and was willing couldn't pick up the scattered chunks of coal that the railroad's firemen weren't about to gather themselves and shovel back in their burners. And I expressed that incomprehension as directly as I could when Avi and I stood awkwardly in front Judge Ben Lindsey a few minutes later, the robed and bespectacled jurist looking like some sort of wizard, it seemed to me, as he gazed downed down at us from the bench.

You see, this is all we were doing, I explained, lifting my bucket and tipping it toward the judge so he could see. It's just scraps of coal, Sir. And when it falls off a train, I'd say it's just finders-keepers.

Oh, you would, would you? And do you suppose we ought to allow every young man to decide for himself which of our laws should be obeyed? The judge seeming willing to spar.

Well, Sir, mostly I'd say the laws make sense. But this one doesn't, and that's the difference. I could feel Avi's elbow, and I ascertained its message. I didn't mean any harm, at least, I added in something of an afterthought.

We both feel mighty bad about this, Avi interjected. I sure won't be out there again, Your Grace.

What about you, Mr. . . . Dumont? I take it you'll be back on the tracks because it seems to you that you should be allowed to be?

I had to think before I spoke this time. Well, Sir, I said after a moment, I don't want to be hauled in again, I can tell you that, so I believe I wouldn't risk it. Besides, you don't get rich off a bucket of coal.

Tell me. What can you sell that bucket for? Lindsey was curious despite the press of a busy docket.

I keep the bucket, of course. It's just the coal I sell. I mean, *would* sell if it was mine to sell, is what I mean. But in this weather, a fellow can get fifty cents for it, easy. You see, there's lots of people that just get by day to day. They don't have big coal bins that a truck or wagon fills up like lots of people.

I realize that, said the judge. And you get by day to day, yourself, I imagine.

I try, Sir, but on days like today I get hauled in for trying.

Judge Lindsey had to stifle his smile with a quick cough. Then he pronounced his sentence. This court finds you both guilty as charged. Neither the tracks nor those seemingly insignificant pieces of coal are public property, and in the eyes of the law you are guilty of both criminal trespass and theft. Yet this court can't help but be reminded that seventy-nine men died in a coal-mine explosion in this state this week, and it views your pursuit of the stuff as being rather benign by comparison. Each of you is sentenced to sixty days in the state reform school, but those sentences are suspended if you agree to enroll in public school no later than tomorrow.

Oh, I can read and write, Your Grace, Avi announced, as if to explain that there wasn't a need for school.

Me, too, I chimed in. I've been to school for a lot of years.

I see. And do you realize that the law requires young men to remain in school until they're sixteen? Neither of you looks sixteen to me.

Seventeen, Sir, just yesterday, I said, lying about my age, as had become my habit. I'm small is all.

Yes . . . yes, I see you are, Judge Lindsey said.

ALTHOUGH I KEPT watch for him, I didn't encounter Avi when I returned to the tracks the following day in search of coal sherds, and this time I scouted as well for railroad dicks, whom I presumed would be on the prowl still for hardened criminals like myself. But if they were out in that arctic weather, I successfully avoided them this time, and I filled my bucket in only an hour and a stroll of a couple of miles, selling its contents to a cattle drover I met on Wynkoop Street, a shivering bohunk who said he'd come to the city in December and by now had squandered his summer wages.

But the dicks did find me the following week, chasing me across a trestle that spanned the frozen South Platte, making me abandon my bucket to the ice-clogged river as they caught up to me, a big and stinking fellow holding me by the collar as I protested that he couldn't take me to court without some evidence, insisting between hard breaths that the dick was wasting his time.

Don't need no damn evidence, the man countered, the breath that smelled of whiskey and rotten teeth a hot wind in my frozen face. You ain't even supposed to be out here. That's crime enough.

Let's chill the little turd off, suggested his partner, still gulping in air after the chase. How about we dump him in the river and teach him a lesson of our own and forget the fucking court?

The big one liked the notion the moment he heard it, and he squeezed me into a bear-hug and tried to hoist me over the wooden railing, screaming at his partner to get hold of my flailing and fighting legs, my hard kicks landing on the winded man's face and chest before at last he pinned my legs, the two men lifting me over the rail like a grain sack and simply letting me go, letting me tumble the ten feet down to the floating ice and shockingly frigid water.

You get the idea? the stinking man shouted down at me before he and his partner turned and strolled away. You don't have no fucking business on these tracks.

I had *never* been that cold, I was sure by the time I lurched and stumbled my way to the shore. I had retrieved my coal bucket, at least, but my boots and trousers and heavy coat and cap were soaked, and I could barely breathe. I scrambled up the river's embankment, the water squishing out of my socks as I took each step, and I trotted to try to warm myself as I made my way to Union Station, where I kept trousers and a second pair of shoes cached in a locker. But I didn't have a spare shirt at the moment, and fellows who lived like I did certainly couldn't keep an array of coats, and neither did it seem a likely bet that I could loiter half-naked inside the station for a day or so without stirring up other trouble.

A Negro shoeshine named Carl I had been friendly with for a long time offered me a towel in the gents' toilet, and I was able to dry my hair, at least, and wring out my wet clothes before I had to put them on again, telling the dark and angular man the truth when he asked where in the hell I'd tried to drown myself, Carl spitting into a can before he responded to my blurted story, telling me he supposed there was no damn end to folks who liked to show how they tough they were. Half the men I shine for is decent people, he told me. The other half wants to feel like they got a slave at they feet for a few minutes much as they want the shine.

Although I wasn't sure I should trouble her, I realized that perhaps I could trade some cleaning work at Big Tess's hotel for a few hours of respite while my clothes dried and my skin and bones struggled back to temperature. I could hang what was wet in the basement on the rack she kept beside the boiler, and if there was any luck at all to be had that day, she might even have hired her cleaning done already and would insist that I sit in her tub instead. When I knocked on the front door of the narrow building on Market Street, which Big Tess kept ritually locked, it was opened almost instantly by Tessa Randolph herself, saying farewell to a small, broad-faced Arapaho woman with a purple knot where an eye should have been, a woman who also came by regularly to clean, I knew, Tessa pressing coins into the woman's plump palm, instructing her not to go off and swallow all the money she'd made.

Good Christ, you look like a drowned rat, Tessa said when her attention turned to the shivering figure on her doorstep. What happened?

Some toughs landed on me over by the Elephant Corral, I said, inventing off the cuff, although I certainly didn't have to lie to her. They took what money I had and threw me in the creek. I thought maybe I could clean for you while I dried out, but . . .

Well, you'd probably be quite a hit around here if I let you clean in your all togethers. But Flossie done did all the cleaning I had. You have a fit, too?

No, not so far.

Well, get in here. It's bitter cold.

Yes, Ma'am, it is.

I tell you what. Tessa rested her hands on her enormous hips. Take all them wet things down cellar and hang them by the boiler. Everything you got on. Then scamper up the back stairs to my tub and clean up a little. Won't be the first time I've had a naked man loose in this place. Shouldn't be nobody using it now.

Suddenly it seemed to me that I was awash in luck, that Big Tess must have known what I'd come hoping for, and I thanked her effusively before I hurried downstairs to follow her instructions. Yet climbing four floors as naked as a newborn wasn't the simplest stunt I'd ever attempted, even if I could use the back stairs where no one was likely to see me. It wasn't so much the nakedness itself that made me uneasy as I began my bounding climb; it was the fact that my business had shrunk to about the size of a grocer's pencil because of the cold, and I cupped my hands in front of myself as I negotiated the dusty stairs and then walked the length of the third-floor hallway, where an encounter seemed far more likely.

Big Tess's bedroom door was open when I reached it; the adjacent receiving room—where she entertained men with a taste for amplitude—was empty; but the light was on in the bathroom, and I could hear someone singing softly through the door that stood ajar. I moved quietly to the place where I could peer through the slit at the door's hinges, and what I saw nearly buckled my knees. Yet it wasn't the onset of a fit that I felt welling inside me this time; it was a far more catholic and carnal kind of sensation, one that mesmerized me and kept my eye pressed to the narrow opening.

Inside the tub in Big Tess's bathroom sat the most beautiful woman I had ever seen. Her auburn hair was piled on top of her head and held fast with a clip. Her shoulders were round and smooth, her fair skin was red from the water's warmth, and her small, dark-nippled breasts seemed to float on its sudsy surface. The woman sang in a language I didn't understand, but I loved the sound of her singing, and although I knew I shouldn't watch, I somehow *had* to, my business suddenly as big as it ever was and cradled in my hand. Hours passed, or perhaps only seemed to, before at last the woman reached for a towel and stood, beads of water falling away from her in little cascades, her body wet and glistening in the soft electric light, her white hips curving out from her waist and the dark thicket of hair between them dripping water until she pressed her towel to it, her buttocks round and perfect when she turned to replace a bottle on its shelf, or so they seemed to be from the place where I intently watched them.

Then, suddenly it seemed, the woman stepped out of the tub and took two steps and pushed open the door into Tess's room. I was momentarily concealed as the door swung wide, but then all too obviously there I stood beside her, the woman turning toward me as if to greet a passerby, casually wrapping the towel around her as she did, her reaction to me neither surprise nor fright.

Are you the next for the bath? she asked. When I couldn't respond, she inquired in a voice both soft and wistful, You're the little fellow who cleans for Tessa, aren't you? I'm Mrs. Kelly.

Yes, Ma'am, I said, although even those words wouldn't come out of me easily, and I tried to conceal with my hands what I no longer could. She told me to leave my wet things in the basement and come up and have a bath, I stammered. I didn't . . .

Well, jump in, Honey. Have my water if you want it, the woman told me dreamily and entirely at ease, her words sounding slow and sweet and lazy, spoken out of what it seemed to me must be a bathing fog.

THIS WAS THE way life would go, I guessed, if I continued to haunt the streets and alleys: on a day when a couple of ugly thugs would dump me in the drink just because I was trying to make a dollar, I also would watch a wonderful woman bathe and she wouldn't seem to mind. One day I'd meet a fine fellow like Avi, who knew a thing or two and who shared my dream of soaring, and the same day I'd end up pleading penitence to a juvenile judge in order to stay out of jail. For every time I luxuriated in Big Tess's tub, I would wash twenty nights in a cracked sink at Union Station. For every beer a stranger bought me, I would meet five toughs who'd try to corner me to strip my pockets. Week to week, month to month, there would be many days when I would feel both fit and fine—neither too lonely nor too trapped by crowds; poor, yes, but heady with prospects, adrift from my family but nonetheless a member of the larger metropolis now.

And there would be other days that would dawn bleak and dark—occasional days when my heart was down in a hole for no reason I could think of—many more days when my head would hurt and my eyes would ache and utterly refuse to focus, days when an enveloping dullness would be all there was in the world to feel, nights and days rent by spells that would leave me wracked and beaten. I would have heady luck on occasion and the world would be my oyster—or at least my shiny scrap of coal—but life would let me down as often as not. It would knock me off my feet in many more ways than the fits alone did, and, just as I'd had to back at Becker's Gymnasium, I would have to brace and take its blows.

I MADE MY first appearance in Judge Ben Lindsey's court in the winter of 1911 and was forcibly returned to the bar of justice three more times before that year was out. Once more before the weather warmed, I was caught collecting coal, and that time Lindsey saw no alternative but to send me to the young men's reformatory in the foothills town of Golden for a month—a sentence that I served willingly enough, better fed for those thirty days than any time since I'd been on my own, the reformatory a place where a resident physician named Dr. Lehman expressed genuine concern about the two spells I suffered while I was there. When the doctor learned that I had suffered similar fits for more than a year, he suggested that this surely was a disorder called epilepsy, a word I remembered from the time when my mother had taken me St. Luke's. The fits were caused by a problem in my brain, Dr. Lehman explained, but when I asked whether there was a way to cure them, the physician informed me that there was not, informing me that only bed rest and a life of inactivity could lessen their number.

I don't have the pleasure to lead that sort of life, I told the doctor, and before many more days were out I was active on the streets again, and soon I was back in Lindsey's court as well, this time answering the complaint of a streetcar conductor who claimed I constantly stole rides on his Broadway route. Another time, I was apprehended when a businessman cornered me on Welton Street and swore that the topcoat I was wearing belonged to him. The man insisted to a cop whose attention he flagged that the coat had been stolen two weeks before while he had dined at the Oxford Hotel. But I contended, truthfully, that the coat had been abandoned in the parlor of a women's hotel where I sometimes cleaned. When nobody claimed it after a while, I tried it on, I earnestly explained to the policeman, and it was a little big, but even so it blocked the weather some. I told Big Tess I had it if the fellow ever came back for it.

The Irish cop recognized Big Tess's name, and asked the man if he might, in fact, have left his coat at her establishment. The man snorted that he certainly had not, and his face flushed with affront at the suggestion, and with me still inside the coat he peeled back its collar to demonstrate that his name, L.M. Bowers, was stitched inside.

Give the gentleman his topcoat, Sonny, the blue-uniformed cop said as he saw the evidence, yet there was something that seemed reluctant about the way in which he escorted me up the street to the courthouse. Them richies ought to be careful where they drop their finery, shouldn't they? But you're a fool too, little fellow, for wearing the thing just like you bought and paid for it.

Judge Lindsey responded in much the way the policeman did, expressing more concern about the fact that I was frequenting a women's hotel than he did about the pilfering of the coat. How many times a week are you there to clean? he wanted to know.

Two, three maybe. Big—Mrs. Randolph—there is always square with me, and it's work I'd do every day, but I'm just one of a few that she likes to have clean for her. I think she wants to pass her charity around.

Yet it isn't charity if you actually work for it, is it? What time of day are you there?

Morning always.

Never in the evening or late at night?

It's too busy that time of day for cleaning, I explained. She wouldn't have it.

No, I suppose not, said the judge, before he announced that in this instance the court found the defendant Thomas Dumont not guilty of the theft of a woolen topcoat that belonged to Mr. L.M. Bowers. Then he had a question: What kind of a chance is there of your actually finding some good and wholesome employment somewhere?

Good, Sir, of finding it, I answered. It's the keeping of it that's the trick. I have these fits, you see. It's a thing called epilepsy, and I have spells out of the blue that lay me low. I've had a good job or two, but the men I worked for wouldn't abide the fits.

It was April 1912—only a couple of days after news had reached Denver that the ship *Titanic* had sunk in the north Atlantic, but that Mrs. Margaret Brown, a local socialite and longtime friend of my mother, had been spared and had, so the papers contended, saved many others as well—when once more I was brought to Lindsey's court. An hour earlier on that morning, a stout and wheezing policeman had seen me crawling out of an alley window at Brown Mercantile. I hadn't robbed the place, as far as the cop could ascertain, but I'd broken the window's glass and damaged its sash, and a warehouseman who had walked out on the loading dock had maintained that this certainly wasn't the first time he'd seen the me loitering on the premises.

When Judge Lindsey asked me—my eyes red and swollen and squinted tight to block out even the courtroom's dusky light—to explain my trespass and the damage to the window, I was slow to speak: I had a fit last night, Sir, a walloper. It happened in the Gents at the train station. There's a colored shoeshine there who's good to me, and he must have stuck with me while I was bad, but when I came to I felt real poor. My head hurt something awful and I couldn't stand the light, which happens sometimes. Carl tried to get me to sack out on a waiting bench, but it's bright in there all night. I couldn't stand it. I had to try to sleep, and I knew Brown's would be dark, and it's just across the street. There's a room full of tack and saddle blankets where you can make a good bed. That's all. I mean, that's the whole of it. I rubbed my eyes with my hand.

And you didn't mind vandalizing the window on your way in? the judge inquired.

I'm sorry about the window. Used to be, you could get in and out without any problem. They must have tightened it up, and I needed someplace quiet so bad that I guess I tore into it.

Yes, I believe you did, Judge Lindsey noted before he declared a recess in the morning's motley parade of juvenile offenders and asked me to meet with him in his chambers.

The judge removed his robe before he sat at his desk, and he responded with a curt and scolding *no* when I asked if by chance he had a smoke. I can't imagine smoking helps you feel any better, he said, as his hand directed me toward an overstuffed chair.

Oh, but it does, Sir. A good smoke always helps. Don't ask me why.

I suppose I was not an ordinary Denver derelict, not one of the typical teen-aged toughs to whom the judge attended every day. Likely, I stood out from the sordid crowd of ne'er-do-wells in several ways, yet surely it was my spells that made me unique in Lindsey's experience, and now the judge wanted to know whether they had been responsible, in fact, for sending me out on the streets in the first place.

They started right after I fell off my father's car. That's two years ago. I banged my head up, and that has to be why they started, but Dr. Locke always swore to my father it was something else.

Galen Locke? He was your family's physician?

Still is, I suppose. He's a big round fellow with bug eyes.

Yes. And he's about to lose his license to practice medicine, from what I hear, the judge told me, then checked himself as if to rein in further gossip. But Lindsey did try to coax more information from me about my past, my parents, the reasons I'd left home and their response to my departure, and he wanted to know, too, whether my parents and I might ever be reconciled. But I was reluctant to answer in other than perfunctory ways, telling the judge only that it was my father who hadn't been able to abide the fits, and who had sworn to my mother that either he or I had to go, telling the judge I moved on mostly for my mother's sake, yet choosing not to mention the abuse or the blows she suffered. I just thought there'd be less trouble if I wasn't there, I offered.

I've met your father, Judge Lindsey told me. I met him and your mother once at a gathering at Maggie Brown's. Awful business about that ship going down, isn't it? I suspect that he can be quite demanding. Do you think he'd like to have you back?

I shook my head. No. I don't suppose so. He and Roger, my brother, they do fine together.

And your mother?

Oh, she'd still have me, I bet. But it would make things hard for her. I'd like to see her though. I will sometime.

The judge wanted to know more as well about how I spent my days, and with the change of subject I was willing now to be candid, telling the judge—who was beginning to seem like a square sort of fellow—about the sites where I slept and the assorted jobs I did, the array of people I'd met and the friends like Avi and Carl I'd made, the way in which Union Station had become a kind of home-base and the respites that Tessa Randolph regularly offered me. Denver was a fine town for a young fellow to get started in, I told Judge Lindsey, and if my spells hadn't hampered me, I figured I'd be set up by now.

You smoke, so I suppose you drink liquor as well?, the judge now wanted to know.

Ale mostly, when I can. But it's dear for a kid like me unless somebody else is buying. Big Tess always has beer for me, and at most any saloon you can always manage one or two if you're clever.

And you *are* clever, I'm beginning to understand. But I doubt you eat very well, and I wonder whether you'd have fewer spells if you took better care of yourself.

I do the best I can, Sir. There's ways to eat.

Judge Lindsey leaned back in his chair before he broached an idea just entering his mind: I suspect you might be clever enough, in fact, to figure out what prompts these spells—whether it's a head full of ale or a day when you don't eat or what have you. This criminal mischief has to stop, let's both agree on that, and perhaps the best thing we can do toward that end is to control your spells. I'll speak with a friend who's a physician—a good one—and we'll see what there might be in the way of medication. You, in turn, will pay careful attention to whatever might trigger them. Agreed?

The doctor at Golden, I can't remember his name, but he seemed pretty sharp, I offered. He said the only thing that would help would be to lay about all day, which I have to do too often anyway. But yes, Sir, if that's what you want.

Before we returned to the courtroom where Lindsey pronounced his judgment—Thomas Dumont guilty again, my sentence suspended pending ongoing consultation with the court—the judge asked if I would meet him at noon at a stationer's shop around the corner. I knew the place, I said, and when I arrived there, Lindsey already had made a purchase and was waiting for me outside.

A ledger like this is actually meant for keeping account of finances, the judge explained, removing a clothbound book with a leather spine from its paper wrapping. But it's stout, at least, and ought to be able to withstand your jaunting about. I want you to write down exactly what you do, what jobs you have, what you eat and drink, how much sleep you get, and record your spells, of course. Perhaps some connections will emerge. It's worth a try, don't you think?

Standing on the busy sidewalk on Court Place, Judge Ben

Lindsey seemed only a trifle taller in his dark fedora than he did without it, only a bit fuller of frame wearing his handsome topcoat than he did in his dark judicial robe, but for the first time, he smiled widely when he handed me the book, and I couldn't help but think that the judge was being kinder to me by far than he had to be. Take it, he said, seeming to enjoy something about the presentation. Call it a diary. Have go at it. Write everything down.

I KNEW IT was easy to pinch them from the pockets of train conductors as they walked the platforms at Union Station, yet somehow it didn't seem proper for me to begin to write in Judge Ben Lindsey's book with a pilfered pencil, so I went inside the stationer's when the judge departed and splurged on five of them for a nickel. I asked the clerk to sharpen one of them, then made my way back to the steps of the courthouse where I sat down, peeled open the cover of the book and pressed it back until the glue at its spine began to crack. The frontispiece contained an intricately inked design that reminded me of the way the world went dark as a spell began to overtake me and sent me somewhere else. I folded it back, then began to write along the blue-gridded lines on the ledger's first entry page:

Today Judge Ben Lindsey bought this book for me. It is the first present I've had in some time. His aim is for me to put down everything I do so we can figure out my fits. Everything has to do with my fits in a way, but I will try to do what he says. At school I was never was much for figures, but I always did fine at composition, at least as I recall.

IT WAS STRANGELY hard, however, for me to grow comfortable recording the dull events of my days. I couldn't imagine that it mattered, for instance, that I paid for a bowl of porridge for breakfast one morning in the restaurant at Union Station, or that on another day Big Tess offered me a bottle of stout in addition to the two quarters I earned for cleaning. Whether it had to do with embarrassment or simply a natural pull toward privacy, it was awkward in the beginning for me to note with words the place where I spent each night, where I washed or worked or scavenged a pouch of tobacco, where I sometimes awoke in the battering fog that followed a fit and had to decipher where, in fact, I was. For weeks, my entries in the ledger were little more than lists of the foods and beverages I'd consumed and the places where I'd bivouacked, notations of the spells I'd suffered and the times, often two days later, when I got back on my feet again.

But before the summer waned, somehow the simple lists began to appear decidedly more like stories. I discovered, despite my initial hesitance, that telling a tale of sorts about the day just done offered me a curious kind of companionship, as well as a way to make some sense of a day that otherwise was a jumble. And there was something about the judge's injunction that made my storytelling a significant challenge as well, the kind of prod that might show me how much I was capable of, what I could create, despite the fact that I was merely a road kid destined to live a forgettable life. And the truth was that not every day was dull in every way. I discovered that I liked to write about the ripping times I spent with Avi, our impassioned conversations and the certainty that we would fly one day. I enjoyed making note of the famous people I knew or had known—and these days unsinkable Maggie Brown, who always had tousled my hair and called me her Carrot Boy, surely sat at the top of my list. There were days as well like the wondrous one in August of that year when I met Mrs. Kelly again, and she remembered me and made me her friend and confederate, solitary nights when I wanted nothing more than to set down with words what had transpired during the daylight in a way that might keep those events alive:

I'd say it was my imagination, or that I was dreaming or I'd had a new sort of spell, but it must have been real, though it seems more like magic still. It was awful hot and after I cleaned for Tessa I sat on her stoop in the alley where it was shady and drank the cold bottle she'd saved for me. It wasn't noon yet and most of the girls were still in bed, asleep I mean, but then one of them came down the back steps to where I was. She was wearing a silk robe with flowers printed on it, and tiny black slippers, and her hair was pinned on top of her head and then I felt a little faint when I realized it was the woman from Big Tess's bath. She said hello and she said, We've met, haven't we? I told her, Yes, Ma'am, and she said, But as I recall, neither of us was dressed for introductions that day, were we? What's your name?

I told her I felt bad about disturbing her, but she said I hadn't disturbed her, I'd just watched her, hadn't I? I didn't know what to say then, but she told me it was okay, and that if men stopped enjoying the sight of her, she'd be in some trouble. I told her I sure did think she was handsome, and she smiled and said, Well, thank you, like they were the sweetest words she'd heard. She wanted to know where I lived and I said sort of all over, and then she asked where I'd choose to be if I had the means. I told her I'd have to think about that, then she told me she was planning to make a move. She said now that there are telephones everywhere, a working gal doesn't have to live in a place like Tessa's. She said she plans to take a room in a real hotel, the best one she can manage, and make her arrangements with men over the telephone. She said she's getting too old to put up with the sorts who walk in off the street, though she's far from an old lady. You'd ring me for a date, wouldn't you, Tom? she asked, kidding like, but I still couldn't think what to say.

Mrs. Kelly—I remembered her name from the time before—said she was desperate to go for a smoke, and did I want to one too? I said a smoke sounded fine, but at first I didn't understand why we didn't just roll one up and have it there on the stoop. Instead, I followed her and we walked a ways through the alley, where she knocked on a loading door. The woman who opened it was Oriental, Chinese I'd say, and she bowed and smiled a little like she knew Mrs. Kelly but she didn't say anything, she just showed us in. Inside were steps that led down some dark stairs and we followed her to the basement where the light was a little better and where a man was, older than the woman. His hair was tied on the top of his head and he had that Chinaman's mustache. He was happy to see Mrs. Kelly and called her by name, and she told him I was her friend and said we sure were interested in a smoke.

The man said it would be his pleasure in an accent I barely could make out, and he took us to a room with several canvas cots, and a wash basin, lit only with a kerosene lamp. I must have been acting funny because Mrs. Kelly said she didn't realize I hadn't been here before. She said I didn't have to try it, meaning this Chinese smoking, but I told her sure, I wanted to. She pulled two cots kind of close and then she laid down on one of them, and even though the light was low, you could see her fine figure from the way the silk draped across her. I felt strange, nervous I mean, but I took a cot too, and Mr. Chin came in again and he washed our faces with a cool cloth before he lit a big long pipe and held it for each of us. I've smoked lots of stuff, tobacco and coffee and chicory and oak leaves and other, but this was different, sweeter, lighter maybe you could say. I wanted to ask what it was, but I didn't want to be stupid, so I just smoked. He left us alone for a while, then came back and we smoked some more, and by the time he came the third time I kind of got the idea.

Fellows who summer down on the river, some of the bindle men too, talk of puff or what they call boo, which is just hemp, and I've smoked that some. But Mr. Chin's smoke, which I suppose comes from China, well, you couldn't help but notice it was special. It made me feel drowsy, sort of, and neither Mrs. Kelly or I had much to say, but it was dreamy too, day-dreamy, because I was far from sleeping and my thoughts just soared along. What it felt like was that everything was easy and grand and just like it ought to be, and why worry or stew. I liked the feeling a lot, though I don't think I said a thing about it. We didn't smoke any more after a while, but Mr. Chin washed our faces again and our feet even, and I could have stayed down there for the longest time. Maybe an hour or two after we started, when it was time for her to go, Mrs. Kelly got up from her cot and came over to me and she bent down and kissed me on the forehead, just to be friendly like. Her robe came open sort of when she did and those bosoms I'd admired so much that other time now nearly were in my face, and I could smell her and I knew I'd never felt so fine. Honey, I've got things to do, she whispered to me, but she told me to stay as long as I wanted. She said she'd taken care of everything, and I felt bad for a second when I realized I should have paid, but I couldn't feel bad for long because I felt so good, like I was flying and didn't own a care, like a beauteous woman had just kissed me and let me sniff the sweet cologne she'd sprinkled between her breasts.

ISABEL KELLY TURNED forty-one in the winter of 1913, a week before that ugly day when dozens of suffragettes were beaten by jeering crowds as five thousand women marched on the White House, seeking the right to vote in national elections. In the state of

Colorado, in contrast, women had been voting freely for nineteen years, and Denver's legion of prostitutes had become, in fact, the city's most dependable voters—virtually everyone casting her ballot in each election in a *quid pro quo* kind of arrangement with the police department, many hundreds of votes dutifully cast for a specified slate of candidates in exchange for the police's tacit agreement to let the women ply their trade without obstruction. And although she was far from politically minded, I knew that Belle was determined indeed to vote Republican as the city's elective offices were contested that year.

Like everyone else in her much-defamed profession, she had been outraged when a local cadre of progressive Democrats—George Creel, Josephine Roche, Harold Hornsby, and Judge Ben Lindsey foremost among them—had taken it upon themselves some months before to rescue Market Street's fallen women by putting them out of work. Although the crusaders largely had failed in their attempt, dozens of prostitutes had been jailed in the aftermath of raids planned by the district attorney's office and halfheartedly carried out by Denver cops. Belle had been forced to spend a freezing night in a downtown lockup and had fumed as she shivered: What on earth was criminal about the service she chose to render? How could louts of every devilish description cheat and steal and even murder without raising the public's ire, while women whose sole and simple business was the proffering of pleasure and a moment or two of escape were branded by Lindsey and his do-gooder gang as society's dregs? Belle Kelly had no doubt that she would far prefer to work on her back for a living than be some rich man's washerwoman solely to salve the prudish conscience of the little judge. She hadn't come to prostitution by the most direct of routes, yet it was work that suited her, she long since had decided, work she was willing to do if the goddamn Democrats would simply leave her and her sister girls of the line alone.

She had been born Mary Isabel Dorothy Dowling in County Clare but had moved to Dublin with her family while still a girl. This she seemed to take a kind of nostalgic pleasure in telling me while we wiled away a snowy autumn night on which she did no business. She was ten when her father was killed while trying to smuggle American rifles into Ireland in support of the Republican struggle. Her mother, a housemaid for an English businessman, died of what was labeled exhaustion when she was seventeen. A year later, she married Jack Kelly, a stevedore's son, on the day before she and her new husband boarded a ship for Boston and an escape from poverty and the rising Irish conflict. But Boston seemed bleak and forbidding during the long winter of 1890, and although friends from home encouraged them to stay, certain that good work would arrive with the spring, the Kellys continued to move westward, settling briefly in Buffalo, Youngstown, and Joliet before arriving in Denver in 1895, still in search of the opportunity they were sure had been cached somewhere for them in America.

A dim sawdust saloon on Larimer Street called the Rose of Sharon at first seemed to be only one more in a long and often-sordid series of stopping-points when Jack went to work there as a barman. But its owner, Cormac Collins, an aging immigrant who longed for Ireland still, and who was charmed by the robust émigré and enchanted by his beautiful wife, made Jack his manager in short order and he introduced the young couple to the larger community of Irish immigrants who made up St. Leo's parish. A week after Collins died of a heart attack on Independence Day, 1897, Jack and Belle Kelly were astonished to learn that the Rose of Sharon had been bequeathed to them.

Denver saloons seldom were places where fine women were welcome, nor were they venues into which many desired to venture, but Belle Kelly was determined to work alongside her husband as they assumed ownership of the Sharon—mucking out the place every morning and keeping its cellar stocked, boiling the eggs and baking the pasties that they offered free with every bucket of beer. The days were long and the work was relentless; Belle suffered unflappably the insults and lewd advances that customers too-often aimed at her, and she was watching from behind the bar on the August day in 1898 when, as Jack was attempting to escort a swaggering troublemaker out of the noisy Sharon, he fell to the filthy sawdust, a buck-knife pressed into his heart.

For half a year, Belle tried to sustain the Sharon and the heady dream she had shared with Jack. But absent him, business fell off and debts mounted alarmingly; one by one, breweries began to refuse to deliver kegs unless she presented cash on their arrival. Without Jack, the work was overwhelming, and life lost all its luster. When a saloonkeeper named Pat Hamrock, whose Arms of Erin stood across the street, offered Belle a hundred dollars if she would simply close her doors and walk away, she sadly acquiesced. She divided the money among her several creditors, cleared her few belongings from the cold-water flat above the bar, then abandoned the Rose of Sharon.

It was Tessa Randolph who noted the young woman wrapped

in packing blankets sleeping in the alley behind her rooming house on the succession of wild and celebratory nights that marked the century's turn, and it was Tessa who had insisted on the frozen night of January 2, 1900 that Belle Kelly come inside and bathe and share her bad-smelling bed, and it was Tessa, as taken with Belle's beauty as the boys in the Rose of Sharon had been, who, after a week of charity, offered Belle a bed and a room of her own if she wanted to have a go at the business of being an evening entertainer, a brief companion, a whore.

Well, I haven't the heart of gold, I'm afraid, Belle told the enormous woman to whom she already felt a substantial debt. But I suppose I'd try it, at least. For a day or two. Do tell me, though, that they're gentlemen, every one.

Oh, bless their hearts, they're darling boys, Tessa told her with a laugh. And them that isn't I beat the bloody shit out of.

That was how Belle's career in the brothel began, how she found a home of sorts on Market Street, a place where she stayed for nearly thirteen years, forging an alliance with Tessa over time that took on the feel of family, forging friendships with some of the women and a few of the frightened girls with whom she stood for selection night after tedious night, making friends as well with one or two of the local fellows who wanted only her, accepting their urgent adorations as if they were gifts of sorts, listening attentively to their plans and their oceans of problems, kissing their cheeks as they went away, telling them, honestly, that she looked forward to their return.

But too much of the time, the men who pressed themselves on top of her, stinking of work and smoke and liquor, were men both young and old who solely sought out the release they had to have, and who otherwise were timidly afraid of women—or who somehow hated them. Some were foul and ugly and obscene, others refused to utter a word as they rutted their way to their finish; and neither the anesthetic of alcohol nor the bliss of opium could make those encounters anything other than the base bargains they were—a service rendered solely for the five dollars it put in the drawer. It was her weariness with the sorts of men who might as well have been pounding into a slab of liver bought from a butcher that at last pushed Belle to try something novel and to leave the place that was both brothel and home.

Although Tessa, grown as wide as her doorway in recent years, tried her best to discourage her, Belle was optimistic that she could survive solely on the income provided by her regular gents—men of some means, of course—fellows who adored her dark hair and pearlescent skin, her prefect small breasts, her other-worldly air and her theatrical enthusiasms. She paid a month's rent for a room she liked in the St. Elmo Hotel in October 1913, had a telephone installed, and on a day when the city's newspapers were fat with stories about the onset of a coal-miner's strike near Trinidad, she placed small ads in the boisterous *Post*, the sensible *News*, and the crusading *Express*:

Mrs. Isabel Kelly of County Clare, Ireland and long of Denver now, loving widow of John Kelly, is in residence at the St. Elmo Hotel, Seventeenth and Blake streets, Telephone TAft 0623. She sends her many friends and acquaintances her kindest regards. The ad was brazen, of course; its purpose was all too transparent and it engendered some risk with the muckraking crowd, but there was something, too, about placing the advertisement that felt free and hopeful and fresh with possibility, like the long-ago day when she and Jack had opened the doors of the Rose of Sharon, a place that had been theirs alone to thrive with or to fail.

IT WAS MRS. Kelly who scolded me and said I had to go see my mother. She said if she was her lad she'd have died of worry by now, and though I told her I'd written letters she said it wasn't the same. I helped her move her things from Big Tess's to her new hotel, and up in her room when we were done she said I should call her Belle, and she told me all about her life, and then she wanted to know about me. I told her everything I could think of, and she seemed interested that my father's a banker, but I suppose it's because it's men in his sort of league that she depends on to do her business. I told her he was a son of a bitch, as a matter of fact, and Mrs. Kelly, well, Belle, was the first person I ever told about the way he treats my mother, and she said if that was the way things were, didn't I have to see her and make sure she was still all right?

What I did finally was telephone from the call-box at Union Station, and it was funny that I had to think what the number was. I was praying she would answer when the operator put the call through, but when it was Anne-Marie, I tried to ask for Mrs. Dumont like I was some business fellow or maybe Father McHenry calling, but I wish now that I would have clicked off. My mother seemed shocked at first, and then I could tell she was kind of crying, and she tried to ask about everything all at once, but mostly she wanted to know if I was okay and I told her I was. She asked if she could see me and I was real nervous about that but I said sure, though I didn't know where.

When I told her where I was calling from, she said in that case, why didn't she meet me in the dining room at the Oxford Hotel in an hour. I told her I didn't really have a good suit of clothes, but she said it didn't matter, and she must have hugged me for fifteen minutes when I saw her step out of a cab and walk over to say hello. She looked both changed and exactly the same, it's hard to describe. She's plumper, but still so pretty, and for the longest time she couldn't stop the tears. We had tea and cake but she didn't seem hungry, and every time she asked about where I lived or worked or whatever, I tried to ask about her or my brother instead. He still boxes, she said, and I guess they say he's good, though he hasn't grown as large as my father would like. She said my father's the same except not quite so cross anymore. I told her I hoped that meant he didn't strike her, and she couldn't talk for a minute, but then she said she realized after I took off that if I was brave enough to do what I did, then she had to be strong enough to tell him no more. She told him that if he wanted them both at home in that house then there could be no more hitting, and though he hadn't said anything, he must have heard her because since then he'd let her be.

She said maybe it would be fine for me at home again too, but I said no, I was out on my own now, and besides, I still had the spells, which were called epilepsy, I'd found out, and then she cried again. I told her I did fine, even so, but she made me promise I'd stay in touch from now on, and why didn't I come to the house on Saturdays while the Rogers were at the gymnasium. She gave me ten dollars, which maybe I shouldn't have taken, but I did, and said I had to let her help me out a little. She said any Saturday, every Saturday, I should come by, and I told her I'd tried to, and it sure made me feel fine to see her.

But what I learned today when I finally got up the guts to knock on the back door was that my father found out she saw me the other day, and he raised holy hell. Anne-Marie was so excited to hear about her meeting me that she let something slip in front of him, and I guess he swore like hell that if she ever saw me again, she'd be the next one out in the street. He put the fear of God in

Anne-Marie and the others, too, that they'll be gone in a snap if they ever try to keep any secrets, but he held his fists to himself this time, which is something, I suppose.

Hearing about it makes me wish I hadn't called her at all, and that Belle had let me attend to my own business. Seems like I can't help but cause my mother grief, though she said she wants me to come back next Saturday regardless of the risk, and she begged me not to disappear again, and I don't know what to do.

I DID NOT return to Tessa Randolph's to clean as often as I had in the past now that Belle lived at the St. Elmo. But Big Tess's remained the women's hotel to which I preferred to bring my occasional customers—men newly arrived in town and in search of some carnal companionship whom I would meet at Union Station and escort to Market Street for a fee. The first time I showed an eager man from Omaha the way to Tessa's, it seemed to me that I'd hit on the perfect occupation, and I tried for a time to meet as many trains as I could each day. Yet the problem, I soon discovered, was that a redheaded urchin in tattered clothes who didn't appear a day beyond his sixteen years wasn't the first fellow whose confidential information traveling men were likely to seek out. And neither could I hold up a card that read WHOREHOUSE ADVICE or some such advertisement. The best I could do, in fact, was loiter near Carl's shoeshine stand, where delicate queries often were made, then offer to be of service. And it was curious that whenever a well-dressed fellow—one with shined spats and an expensive valise and a hat that bespoke his sense of style—would tell me he had the funds for a rendezvous with a beautiful woman, the man insisting, in fact, on a gal who was kind of classy, I never broached Belle Kelly's name, despite the way in which my silence cut into my profits.

Lately, Avi Sokolow had jockeyed his irregular work at Ira Humphreys's machine shop into something of a steady job, and it was Avi who had suggested that perhaps the wealthy entrepreneur might have work for me as well. On a warm, winter-defying day in December 1913, I hopped aboard a crowded Seventeenth Street streetcar and ably avoided its conductor en route to Broadway, then transferred to a trolley that was southbound to Alameda, where Humphreys's brick garage was wedged among the array of car dealers and manufacturers who had turned Broadway, once a stately, tree-lined boulevard, into a flourishing gasoline alley.

Tall and angular at twenty-three, and very proud of his thin mustache, Humphreys was the eldest son of Colonel A.E. Humphreys, a West Virginian who had become wealthy beyond imagining in Oklahoma's Blackwell oil field, and who, together with his large family, now anchored Denver society. Yet although young Ira Humphreys—called Bumps by everyone—did fancy horses and sartorial style in ways that befit his wealth, his passions were nuts and bolts and machinery with moving parts. He had endured only a year of mechanical engineering at the University of Colorado before he established his own machinery company, designing and manufacturing water pumps and irrigation equipment but dabbling as well in the romance of the motorcar. Horses belonged on racetracks and polo fields, not on the streets anymore, Bumps Humphreys declared to Avi and me as the three of us stood admiring the sleek silver automobile that was nearing completion in his cluttered and sun-splashed shop, the first car Humphreys had built by hand.

Motorcars will be all you see in a year or two, he told us. Pastures will be full of retired teams and you'll have to hunt to a find a fresh turd on a city street. But they're just the passing thing. About the time you two take on families, everybody will have an airplane of their own. That's the logical way to travel; no roads to build or get muddy or fill up with snow. People will travel in the sky as much as on the ground.

Wow, I said. But I'd sure love to drive this down Broadway in the meantime.

Oh, this isn't a runabout, Humphreys explained. Wouldn't think of risking it. Now that the Ford plant is busy up the street, there'll soon be more Model Ts than you'll believe, about half of them out of control, I'd imagine. This is a racing machine, built just for speed. I call it September Morn, because it's all stripped down, like the painting. Bumps Humphreys winked at the two of us, and I understood the ribald reference if Avi, it seemed, did not.

Bumps is going to run it in a race just before Christmas, Avi explained to me. Cheyenne to Denver. A hundred miles and he'll make it in half a day.

I'd better make it in about three hours or I'll be sucking the hind tit. Bumps found the wrench he wanted, then bent into the motorcar's open hood to return to work.

Say, Bumps, Avi said to try to hold his attention a moment longer. The reason Tommy came round today is he's my good pal and a regular working guy. I told him we was real busy around here and that you might have some work for him.

Humphreys stood again, towering above us, and he seemed to take my measure before he spoke. Well, there might be some from time to time. You know anything about this kind of work?

Not exactly, Sir, but I catch on quick, and I'd show up real regular.

Him and me met watching the Birdman back when, Avi explained. He's crazy for aviation like I am. Except he has these spells, where he blacks out, so I tell him I'll have to do the flying for both of us.

My irritation was instant, and evident, and as Avi realized what he'd said he tried to muffle the blunder with more in the way of recommendations, but the damage was done.

You mean like epilepsy or something? Humphreys asked. That sort of spell?

Yeah, I said. But not very often anymore.

Even so, don't suppose I'd better risk it. With all this heavy machinery, I'd hate to get you hurt. But you seem like a good chap. You can come round again when we have her finished and take another look. He offered me his hand. What did you say your name was?

Tommy. Tommy Dumont. I'm sure my voice betrayed my disappointment.

I know a chap named Roger Dumont. A little younger than me, older than you. Played some polo with him before I went into business. I hear he's quite the boxer these days.

He's my brother, I said, my tone a bit brighter, as if the fraternal connection might persuade him to reconsider.

But it did not, and he only asked me to say hello to Roger for him before he bent beneath the hood again, Avi lifting his hands to his face and cringing to try to express his regret at how stupid he'd been, but I simply shrugged in response, letting it go because there was nothing else I could do, and because this was far from the first time my fits had cost me an opportunity, leaving Avi to get to the work Bumps Humphreys had for him.

THIS TIME, THE manager at Brown Mercantile wanted the punk who'd broken it to pay for the alley window, and the judge's patience with my ongoing entries into places I didn't belong had reached its limit as well. As he had twice before when I had been brought before him, Judge Lindsey took me into his chambers on a raw morning in April 1914 rather than address me in open court, and the judge had a bit of news for me before he gave me a stern admonishment that was followed by a curious request.

I had a call the other day from a friend who's a physician, the judge said as he rested his forearms on his polished desk, his words delivered rather formally despite the familiar subject they referenced. He's the fellow I asked some time ago whether there was any medication for your condition. Well, it seems that at last there is. I wrote it down. It's called Luminal, and they don't dare give it to children, but from what I understood, it quiets the brain somehow. According to him, it's been used sparingly for a year or so, and although it makes people drowsy at first, many who're taking it have far fewer convulsive attacks.

I'm seventeen now, I told him, honest about my age for the

first time since I'd known him. But I'd hate being sleepy all day, even when I hadn't had a fit. And anyway, it'd have to be pretty dear.

I might well offer to pay for it myself, if it would help keep you out of this court. Do you suppose you could accept a bit of charity?

I guess I'd have to think about.

Well, while you do, you should consider, too, that you're this far from another trip to Golden. The judge held his thumb and his index finger an inch apart and presented them for my inspection, then informed me that Brown Mercantile wanted its window paid for by the lout who'd broken it, a fair proposition, it seemed to him.

But I was strapped, I told him. The two dollars the window would cost were three more than I could muster at the moment, and I imagined myself captive again in the horse-drawn paddy wagon that had delivered me to the reformatory two years before. Yet instead of meting out a month or two of incarceration, the judge decided to shift the subject, first wondering aloud whether I might do an errand for him instead of serving a sentence in juvenile jail, then openly putting the proposition to me.

It seemed that a coal strike down south had got mean. There'd been some shootings, and from what I could ascertain, the judge was worried that there might be many more. What the judge wanted was for me to take a train to a place called Ludlow, but beyond that his desires weren't specific. He wanted me to look around, that was the gist of it, to write down in my ledger book the important things I saw and to come home with a sense of the situation. Judge Lindsey needed my opinion of things, that was what it amounted to, and I—mindful that a wagon-ride to Golden was the only alternate travel I'd likely be offered—told the judge I'd gladly go.

WE STOPPED IN Colorado Springs to let off some fellows in spiffy clothes who're probably headed for the Antlers Hotel for the night, and I thought for a minute I saw my father. But it wasn't him, so I shoved my heart back up where it belongs, and now Pueblo is behind us too and the train is heading into country that has a desert look about it, though we're coming near to two high and snowy peaks that still seem a lot like Colorado.

I can't figure out why the judge thought I was the best one to send down here. Maybe he just couldn't think of anybody else, or it could be that I'm the only damn fool that would do it, but he needs to find out more than what he can from the papers, and though I can't do much else that's worth anything, I have learned how to keep my eyes open these past years. I believe I can tell a square fellow from a crook real quick, and I know the difference between spinning a good story and telling an outright lie, plus I keep this book these days.

I told the judge I haven't been able to come up with what causes my spells by writing everything down like he hoped, but I keep scribbling anyway. Nobody's read a word of this, and only Belle and the judge really know what I'm up to, though a few like Carl and Avi like to tease me about why I always pack around a ledger book. It's just a habit more than anything now, I suppose, and it passes the time. I don't seem quite so worthless when I write things down. I don't know why.

It'll be different to try to write about people other than me. It sounds more interesting, that's for sure, and though I wish I knew more about what the judge wants me to look for, I'm going try to do a fine job of whatever it is I do, and then write it down just so. It was good of him to send me on this errand instead of off to Golden again, and I'm a fool if I don't make the most of it. I'd like to be more than only a road kid, I really would. If I didn't have these fits I know I could help Bumps Humphreys build motorcars or airplanes or do a hundred other things. But that's the breaks, like they say, and I'll just have to do what

I can. I'm lucky, I know, that I came across the judge and Belle and everyone.
Sometimes I wonder why they're all as fine to me as they are.

The train's pulled south out of Walsenburg now and those two high peaks
do kind of command the world down this way. The sky's big and bright today
and it almost makes you think we'll get some springtime. Sure hope I make a
go of Ludlow.

AS I STEPPED off the train at the clapboard depot on Sunday
afternoon and made the short hike to the miners' camp—wearing
only a tattered waistcoat against the chilly weather—I saw little but
celebration. A feast of sorts had been laid open to the sun between
two rows of tents; stews and breads and potatoes and pans of an
exotic pastry were spread on temporary tables built from sawed
boards and sawhorses; bottles of beer sat soaking in cold-water tubs.

The striking miners wore red bandannas around their necks
during the communal meal, their scarves a sort of uniform, a symbol
of their solidarity, I later learned. Some brandished bandoliers
across their chests, and a few still wore their braces of bullets when
the meal was finished, and a baseball game commenced. Although
the game was alive with the bantering noise of several languages,
the immigrants seemed happily unconcerned about the contest's
rules of conduct, and when a foul ball careened into the clutch
of guardsmen who had wandered by to watch, a great cheer rose
up from the hard-dirt lot, as though the errant ball had scored a
winning run. We'll have your Dago hides tomorrow, I heard one
of the soldiers shout as he threw the ball back onto the field, but

his bold admonition was quickly drowned by jeers, and the crowd's attention returned to the field.

The many-layered and sugar-glazed dessert was the Greeks' contribution to the meal, a small, sloe-eyed Italian woman explained in English as she handed me a plate when the game was done at dusk. Today was Easter, she said, at least according to the Greeks it was, and given the life that Rockefeller had forced on them that spring, two Easters were damn welcome. When I tried to decline her generosity, the woman seemed to scold me. You better take it when it's offered, mister, she insisted. You never know when's the next time you'll eat in Ludlow.

In the swelling darkness, Greek men in short-collared shirts and high boots that held their trousers led the dancing in the soft light of a single fire. There were songs as well, and then an impassioned prayer in Greek, or so I assumed the language was, and although sleeping children had to be lifted from their mothers' laps, everyone stood at last to sing in English a song that openly stirred them, its lyrics insisting that they would rally from the coal mines and struggle to the end.

I made my way back to the depot in the moonless and frigid night and slept inside beside a still-warm stove, my slumber only fitful, an odd, metallic taste in my mouth again, the taste that often meant a spell was about to overtake me. But one had not seized me during that long night, I knew when I awakened in the dawning light to a stir of angry voices. Instead, I had been visited only by dreams—sudden, jumbled, momentary visions of baseball and lumbering trains; an odd image of the judge enveloped by the huge leather chair in his chambers; sounds that were the shouted oaths and pledges of exotic men, and the remembered melody of a song they sung to freedom.

IN THE MINUTES before I feel asleep beside the coal stove, I had sharpened a pencil with my pocketknife, then studiously entered these words on the gridded lines in my ledger book:

People here speak at least a dozen languages, more maybe, but everybody knows some English, I'd say. They tell me the Greeks are only dressed in such a style because today is their Easter Sunday, but they do cut a handsome swath. Many of the men, Greeks, Italians, Mexicans, all types of them, make some show of bullets or have a pistol strapped to their hips. I've seen no rifles yet, but I haven't been invited into anyone's tent. The women all seem tired, more than anything, and the children are happy enough, though isn't that their usual way? I asked a woman who gave me a piece of pie if people were worried about more trouble. She spoke good enough English and said why worry when everyone knew trouble would be along when it was ready.

There are dirty patches of snow here still, and above the bare hills you can see two high peaks a ways off to the west. A man on the train said the Indians call them Huajatolla, *which he said means Breasts of the Earth, and I have to say that you could imagine them as two big bosoms easily enough. They are beautiful and are covered with heavy snow still and I reckon it's awfully cold up there, though likely a little more peaceful than down here in the midst of this distress.*

I COULD NOT hear the words of the conversation as I awoke, but the men's voices were loud and lit with agitation. I scurried to put on my shoes and stuff my blanket inside my rucksack, guessing that someone was being berated for letting me sleep inside the depot. But as two men moved into the small waiting room, it quickly was clear that neither one was concerned about my presence. Instead, the issue seemed to be an angry allegation that the strikers were holding a nonunion miner against his will. A redneck—the man who had led the dancing the night before, I was sure, and whose English was wrapped in a heavy accent—was insisting to a guardsman that the fellow in question had left the colony of his own accord three days before. But the man in uniform—who *had* to be Pat Hamrock, keeper of the Arms of Erin on Market Street, a Denver saloon where I sometimes performed coin tricks for besotted patrons— now was shouting that the man's *wife*, for Christ's sake, had sworn not thirty minutes ago that her husband was being held by the Dagos at Ludlow.

This wife is mistaken, the redneck implored. I tell you only truth. Everyone in camp is there of the free will. I tell you.

Then a second militiaman burst into the room and interrupted them. My God, Major, we're in for it! he shouted. The rednecks are heading for the railroad cut! They aim to pin us down!

Not so! Not so! shouted the redneck, whose eyes now mirrored the alarm on the messenger's face. I am Tikas. I am the leader. They wait to hear of this meeting. There is no fighting!

But from the tall station windows the men and I could see that scores of armed strikers *were* running across the ball field toward the place where the eastbound tracks sliced through a small hill, a cut that would offer them a bit of protection as well as a position, Hamrock immediately understood, from which they could fire on the guardsmen. Horrified by what he saw—a surely disastrous advance that undeniably was underway—Tikas fled from the building and raced toward the strikers, waving his handkerchief high over his head, screaming at the men to retreat to their tents. But no one heeded him as the surge of strikers continued—toward the cut in the east as well as into a shallow arroyo cut at the colony's northern edge.

The Greek leader was frantic, I could see from inside the station, and both guardsmen still in the room were equally troubled now. Pat Hamrock instructed the messenger to return to the hill to order the marksmen to hold their fire before he raced across the tracks to his quarters to try to telephone the guard commander in Denver. Then I was alone in the suddenly quiet station, my bewildered face pressed to its narrow eastern windows, and I watched dozens more men in red bandannas disappear into the railroad cut. I watched frightened soldiers on the nearby hill swing a huge machine-gun and struggle to aim it at the strikers, saw other soldiers fall to their bellies and sight their rifles as well, saw the breathless messenger gain the small hill's summit and disappear. Then, abruptly, all of the plain was alive with the clamor of gunfire.

For a reach of minutes, my fear and complete confusion—the lunacy of what was unfolding and a paralyzing uncertainty about what I should attempt to do in response—froze me at the windows. But this sudden madness was the very thing the judge had cautioned me about—its swelling likelihood had been the reason Lindsey sent me south—and now I knew I had to act quickly, to alert the judge or *someone*, to help somehow, if help were possible. But I couldn't find the fat stationmaster I remembered from the day before, and neither could I see a telephone as I peered through the steel latticework of the ticket window into a tiny office. Out on the waiting platform, the empty tracks that receded from the station in three directions evidenced the truth that no train was arriving to offer timely assistance. Away to the north, however, I could see that the Greek, this man called Tikas, had reached the strikers' tents and was attempting to gather those who remained there—children, women, men who hadn't joined the hurried offensive—and push them toward the safety of the arroyo.

Despite the pops of gunfire that seemed to sound from every direction, I raced toward Tikas and the tents, and there, amid a din of dogs and chickens and the uncomprehending cries of children, I, too, began to make my way from hovel to hovel, tearing open each tent flap, finding no one inside the first three dwellings I approached, then finding a frightened mother and her children in the fourth, pulling them outside, shouting at them to run, *run damnit*, with the others, finding three young women and a dozen terrified children farther down the muddy row, all of them working their way into a large storage pit that had been dug beneath a bed, pulling boards over their heads as they huddled together, ignoring my repeated pleas for them to flee.

I searched four more empty tents before I found other stragglers—this time a family who seemed equally intent on staying where they were, two children lying prone on a steel-posted bed, their parents seated beside them on the mattress, their wan faces blank and unbelieving. You've got to get out of here, I implored, but the man only shook his head in a silent and negative response. Our boy, said the woman, they shot our Frank, and only then did I notice the boy's bloody face, his vacant eyes, his gaping mouth. Bring him, *come on*, I insisted again, but this time the man's response was the long-barreled pistol he raised and halfheartedly pointed in my direction, and I said nothing more before I let the tent flap fall and moved on, running, stooped at the waist to shield myself from the scatter of bullets, now in search of the leader whom the rednecks had not obeyed.

THE SPRAY OF rifle fire that filled the morning lingered into the afternoon. For long minutes, the guns would go silent, only to begin to crackle again in response to a shout or a sudden cry. At noon, guard reinforcements arrived from Trinidad—nearly two hundred now were pressed into battle—and an hour later a party of ten soldiers, crawling north along the ditch that flanked the railroad tracks, made its way to the weathered store and abandoned saloon that stood beyond the station. Protected by the two buildings, the guardsmen raked the railroad cut with fire from the flank and were able to roust the main contingent of strikers and send them running toward a stand of tree-stubbled hills a half-mile away in the east. Four rednecks were hit as they fled, their bodies falling motionless on the plain. A soldier attempting to get still closer to the cut was wounded by a bullet in the neck, then died as his comrades attempted to pull him back to safety.

With the strikers now in retreat, and emboldened by their secure positions and swollen numbers, the soldiers made their way farther north along the tracks toward the colony where Tikas, two fellow union men, and I lay on the plank floor of the UMW's headquarters tent, two rifle barrels piercing holes they had torn in the canvas. When at last I found the Greek leader late in the morning, I realized that Tikas had no idea who I was, armed with nothing more than a slender book. He had told me to stay—and stay low, for Christ's sake—protected a bit by the rough-sawn boards that skirted the sagging tent.

The firing had ebbed to only occasional rifle shots that rang out from an uncertain distance by the time a small contingent of soldiers braved entry into the camp. They were led by an officer whom his subordinates addressed as Major, but this was not Pat Hamrock, I could see through the rip in the canvas. The tall and erect and imposing man—his roughrider's hat cocked back, his uniform pressed and perfect—must have arrived at Ludlow sometime after the fighting commenced, I supposed, and there was something about his steely movement and his sporadic spittle of words that bespoke a seething anger and an impatience to be done with this bloody day. Find his filthy ass, the major barked when a soldier asked him for further instructions. He's still here somewhere and I want him. Tear open every tent if you have to, but *find him!*

Let's smoke him out, suggested the soldier. Let's torch the whole fucking mess.

However you get him is your business, but I want him, *now.* The major—Hornsby, the lieutenant had called him—seemed to be acquiescing to the destruction of the camp without having to order it, and the threat must have chilled the Greek leader who lay crouched at my side.

Stay, Tikas whispered to his men and to me, then he stood, peeled back the canvas flap and stepped into the flat light of the spring afternoon. I am Tikas, he called out to the soldiers, only two tents away. He held his hands in the air and waited without moving as they rushed toward him, seizing him by the shoulders, surrounding him, crushing him with the enthusiasm of their capture.

We got him, Major! one of the men sang out. Fucking Louis the Greek, we got him.

I am Tikas, the Greek repeated as Hornsby approached, a thin smile curling onto the major's face as he surveyed his prey, pushing his small spectacles up on his nose with an extended finger.

So you are. So you are, you bloody Dago bastard.

Take me, but no more. No more fighting.

You should have thought about that before you set your jackals loose, shouldn't you? I lost a fine man to you vermin, and now you'll answer for it.

We have dead also, Tikas answered. Shooting started from the hilltop. I told other officer we have no nonunion man here. We want no fighting.

Hornsby slapped the weary striker with the back of his gloved hand, and the cuff now encouraged his soldiers. Let's string him up, Major. Right now, Sir. We've got some strong rope for the greasy fucker!

We'll let him enjoy a little fire first, said Hornsby. Let him smell the stench of this place as it crackles. You fellows do your business now if you need to.

The major wheeled and casually walked away with that

instruction, as if to separate himself from it, to order the deed done without the need to attach his name and rank to it, and he stood with his hands clasped behind him, his eyes trained on the two high peaks of *Huajatolla* as his soldiers scurried into the task, finding a barrel of coal oil in which they dipped slats and sticks for makeshift torches. Tikas said nothing more and did not strain against the four men who continued to hold him fast. Only a few feet away, the two rednecks and I still lay in paralyzed silence.

The haggard structure on the colony's southwest corner was the first tent they set ablaze, two soldiers—giddy with both malice and their unbridled freedom—holding torches to the canvas for only a moment before it lit like the wick of a candle. Then down the row the two men surged, lighting tents on either side of them, running away from the wild lick of the flames and the immediate heat, others claiming rows of their own now, each canvas dwelling first catching tentative fire then exploding into total destruction only seconds later. New cries came up as the flames rose and thick smoke roiled into the clear spring sky—cries from dumbfounded strikers ensconced in the nearby arroyo, the shouts and oaths of the soldiers themselves, the terror-filled shrieks of the few stragglers still in the burning camp.

Aghast and afraid and still not moving, I could see the family whose son had been shot struggle away from their tent at last as soldiers set fire to its fabric, the boy's limp body draped over the father's shoulder; father, mother, and daughter floundering as they raced to escape the blaze. But I could see no one else, and I heard only muffled cries and the more general noises of madness before the back wall of the tent where *I* crouched suddenly was bright with fire, before my companion rednecks shrieked as they scrambled to their feet, tearing open the flap and rushing headlong into two guardsmen whose pistols were drawn and pointed. I emerged behind them a moment later, my wide eyes etched with panic, but before I could raise my hands in surrender, a soldier seized me and struck me with the butt of his pistol, scraping skin from my scalp and forehead, sending blood spilling into my eyes—this ragtail no doubt just more Dago filth as far as the cursing soldier was concerned, notwithstanding my fair and freckled skin or my red hair that now was knotted with blood.

You . . . you've got it wrong, I stuttered. I'm the fellow you're looking for. I sent my wife to tell you these bastards are holding me here. Bless her, she got me some help.

Major! The guardsman who had hit me called out to Hornsby. This punk here says he's the miner the Dagos are holding.

Hornsby came close and studied me before he spoke. This wife of yours, she have a name?

Same as mine.

And that is?

Samuelson. It was the name I thought I had overheard.

What's her first name?

I call her Dolly.

What's her given name, goddamnit? Hornsby had grown impatient.

Why, Mary, Sir.

Who are you, you little fuck?

I'm Samuelson, Sir, I said a second time before Hornsby's hard fist found my gut and sent me buckling to the ground. The major's boot hit my rib cage and I spun on my hip as I received the blow, but then there were more boots, a quick and stinging sortie of kicks to my head, my belly, my groin, and I pulled my knees to my chest and tried desperately to cover my head before the light went white and very bright and I felt a warm and spreading wetness in my trousers and then I felt nothing at all.

THEY HAD ME down on the ground by then, and I was getting a good beating and I hurt pretty bad, but then I went into a fit and I don't know what happened next. It was dark when I knew something again and I was lying on the ground near the tracks that run to Walsenburg, so I must have been drug there, either by Mr. Tikas and his men or those fellows who were punching me up. I still heard gunshots now and then, and there was crying and moaning over where the camp had stood. The big flames had settled down to smolders, and it stunk bad, and in the light from the embers it looked like the only things left standing were the wood stoves people had used inside their tents. It had been a regular town, sort of, like the early gold camps must have looked, but it was gone now and mostly everyone with it. I could see a few people poking through the ashes, some of them calling out the names of kin they couldn't find, and it was a pretty sad sight, even from off by the tracks.

I don't know why I didn't notice at first, but it startled me when I saw Mr. Tikas and the other men, their bodies, right where I was. I didn't have to check; the way they were lying, it was plain that they were dead. But when I got up I did look at Mr. Tikas real close, though the sight of him made me sick. His head was beat up bad and his neck was sliced open and there were three big bloody holes in his shirt, which had to be from gunshots, though I've never seen one before. Those soldiers had their way with him something awful—and I took him to be a fine man during the time we were stuck in his tent together.

I felt poor, but I thought I should try to see what was going on now, and I stumbled over to the burned-out camp. A few soldiers were there, poking through things, taking a few odds and ends for themselves. Over near the corner, where the first fires had been set, two men, both of them the strikers that they call rednecks, were digging with shovels and pulling away burned boards from under a steel bedframe as fast as they could. They were speaking a language I didn't understand but it was plain that they were frantic to find their people, and it only hit me when they pulled the last of the charred boards away that this must have been the tent where I'd seen the women and their little ones scrambling to get underground.

I haven't seen too much that is awful in my life. I used to think the worst was finding two bindle men whose legs had been sliced off by a train down in the Bottoms. They'd bled to death, and a dog ran off with one of the legs when I walked up the tracks, collecting coal. That stuck with me an awful long time, but far worse than that, I know I'll remember forever the sight of those two women, the same ones I'd tried to get to run, and all those tiny kids in that horrible black hole, slumped together, still as could be. The rednecks and I jumped in there as quick as we could, but there wasn't any use. They weren't burned, any of them, but they were awful sooty and it made me sick again to think how it would be to die like that. I know it was harder for the redneck men because they must have been husbands to the women and fathers to the babies, they way they cradled all of them in their arms. I hated it that I hadn't done more to get them out of there, and I was crying and tried to tell those men that I hadn't helped the way I could have, but they didn't understand me. Then some soldiers came over and pointed their rifles down at us and said if we didn't get the hell out of there that minute there'd be three more dead Dagos. One of the fellows pleaded with them in his own language and he got a rifle butt in the ear for it, and then I climbed out and the rednecks after me. The soldiers made sure we walked away, and it seemed like making those men leave was the worst thing yet, and all they could do was wail and curse God Himself, I imagine, there in that stinking darkness.

IN THE RAILROAD depot at Ludlow in the small hours of the morning, I lay curled on a wooden bench and wished for sleep, although I could not imagine sleeping—despite my exhaustion and the piercing pain and the dull disorientation that always followed a fit—any more than I could trust that the terrible events of the day before actually had transpired. It was a gruesome dream, wasn't it?, one that might, in fact, have been bred by the vapors that had consumed my brain when I'd lapsed into convulsions. Yet one undeniable proof that the events that swirled in my mind were as real as the hard bench on which I lay was the body of the boy Frank Synder—his jaw pressed shut and held with a striker's red bandanna tied round his head, his eyes kept closed with coins—that lay on the bench across from me. The boy's sister shared the long seat, her head on a folded coat near her brother's booted feet, and she, at least, seemed to sleep. The parents—dazed, still stunned, destroyed by their son's senseless death—sat upright, holding hands, saying nothing, hearing as I did the animated conversation of the militiamen who were decamped in the depot's little office, their banter alternately boastful and singed with disgust.

I say a week more and the whole thing'll be over. These thieving Wops and all the agitators sent packing, or sent to hell, men who *want* to work back in the mines. The voice was one I had heard before.

Like you say, Major, the fuckers did it all themselves. Let their camp burn rather than surrender to the authority of the state. They ain't even human, the way I size them up.

But anybody who asks you, all you did when the fire broke out was get as close as you could to see if you could help anybody get out. The same goes for Louis the Greek and those two. Fire broke out, and it was quick and powerful fierce, and then there was hellacious shooting from out of the hills, those rednecks too dumb to know what else to do, I guess. Tikas got caught in their fire, the sorry son of a bitch. Isn't that the way you saw it, Major?

That's the report that needs to be written.

I recognized the voice now and remembered the way Hornsby had turned to look at the two high peaks once he'd told his men to do what they wanted to do. Then I heard his voice again. It's a tragedy. Those women and children locked in that pit all day, out of air to breathe by noon. Long dead by the time the fires started. But goddamnit, this is exactly what happens when these dark races are allowed to run in packs like rabid dogs. It's a tragic thing.

I could hear the men's mumbled agreement, and across from the bench where I lay I could see that Frank Synder's washed cheeks were the color of watered milk and that his hair, combed carefully back, was as blonde as I remembered Major Hornsby's was, and I tried to make note in my weary and sickened and seizure-dulled mind of every detail I would describe to the judge as the terrible pain continued and the night lingered without end.

THE SYNDER FAMILY, their murdered son, and I had boarded a southbound supply train on Tuesday morning and made our way to Trinidad, where sidewalks, saloons, dining halls, and union halls were swollen with frightened and sometimes vengeful citizens, their loud conversations laced with rumors of *hundreds* of deaths the day before, Frank Snyder's body borne in his father's arms through the tumultuous streets to the Hall and MacMahon mortuary as the first proof in the mining town that the much-rumored violence fifteen miles to the north had been both real and deadly.

At the Toltec Hotel, I tried to telephone Judge Ben Lindsey in Denver, but my battered appearance, together with the general unease that hung in air like coal smoke, were enough for me to be turned away by a haughty and nervous desk clerk despite the dollars I proved to have in my possession. At the office of the *Chronicle-News*, however, a young secretary willingly placed my long-distance call, but the judge was in court at that moment, and I had to leave a sketchy message with his secretary, which distressed me. Tell him Tommy Dumont telephoned, I said with some hesitation to the faint male voice that crackled in the earpiece. Tell him I called from Trinidad, and that there has been bad trouble at the strike camp. Tell him I'll keep a watch out like he asked, but that I have no notion what else to do.

In a driving rain on Thursday, however, I agreed—despite my misgivings and no little amount of fear—to return to Ludlow. I had walked to the mortuary after breakfast, hoping someone there would know where Frank Snyder's parents were, and my inquiry had led an undertaker to turn some questions back to me. Had I been with them at Ludlow? Did I know where all the dead lay? Would I accompany this spindly man whose mustache concealed his lips to retrieve the many bodies?

I can tell you right where they are, I offered instead.

Would five dollars persuade you to show me, little man? the undertaker asked.

If the soldiers recognize me, I'm afraid I'll be in for more than they already gave me.

You can hide in the hearse if you want to. If you're along, I can save myself the looking and be quick about getting out of there myself. I wouldn't go at all except it's sheriff's orders.

Although the money did not lure me like it otherwise would have, at last I agreed to go—in largest part because the judge's injunctions crossed my mind again—and en route to the ruins of Ludlow I rode inside the horse-drawn hearse for protection from the rain as much as the wary eyes of the soldiers. But the scene at the camp—mired in soot and muck and a stink far worse than I remembered—was ghastly in the dripping daylight, and as soon as I saw it I was sure that the judge would not have pressed me to return. Groups of soldiers in water-slick dusters, the wide brims of their hats bent by the rain, huddled together with nothing to do, four of them near the pit where the bodies lay, the grisly hole now filling with gray water. As the undertaker began his grim and laborious task—pulling the soaking bodies from the pit, wrapping each one in a canvas tarp, stacking them like firewood inside the wood-frame hearse, I pulled the topcoat I'd liberated the day before from a rack at a Trinidad restaurant tightly across my chest, and I did my best to tuck my head inside it as well when I climbed up onto the hearse's driving seat and into the full force of the rain.

The bodies of Louis Tikas and his men appeared more cruelly contorted than when I last had seen them in the smoky darkness, and something else had changed by the time the hearse drew near them: each man's red bandanna had been untied from his neck and now was stuffed in his open mouth. I was sick when I saw it, watching the undertaker attend to the last of the ugly task, my thin vomit staining my coat and spreading onto the cracked leather seat of the hearse, and the tall man and I were soaked to our bones by the time we returned to Trinidad at dusk with our bitter cargo.

I'VE READ ALL the papers while the weather has been so bad, and mostly they've got it right, though the fellow who reports for the Express *is the only one who seems to care about what's happened. The last four nights I've spent at a rooming house near the river, which runs in a torrent now. It's cost me two dollars each time, and though that's pricey, I figure I'm still on the judge's errand, and I'm feeling kind of poorly still from the beating and the fit.*

Town seemed like a city today with so many people arriving for the funerals. And for a while it looked like there'd be more bad trouble when a fire started at the mortuary. They'd pulled all the caskets out into the street by the time I got over there, and the fellows from a hook and ladder squad got the fire out before the building went up, but it sure put everybody's nerves on edge. The fire wasn't an accident, that's for certain, but all the talk in the street so far is only guesswork about who might have done such a thing. It was late getting started, but there was a funeral mass at Holy Trinity for all the children and the two mothers, neither much older than me, then two drays drawn by black horses

carried the coffins to the cemetery, two black coffins and eleven little white ones,
and it seemed like everybody who watched them pass was as choked up as I was,
yet the difference is that I have to contend with knowing that I could have helped
keep them alive. The body of the Snyder boy, and his family with him, went by
train to Missouri, their fares paid by the union, a friendly fellow told me, and I
wish I would have had the chance to say so long.

It was afternoon and the rain broke a bit before hundreds, thousands
maybe, were out again for Mr. Tikas's funeral. Only a few were allowed into the
mortuary for the service, done in Greek, I'd imagine, and I heard some talk that
the men inside the chapel had their rifles with them and swore revenge before they
closed his coffin. It was the same two horses, I'm sure, but this time they pulled
a fancy hearse with gaslights on the side and smoked-glass windows, and behind
it, all the way down Commercial Street and across the river and up the hill to
the Knights of Pythias cemetery men marched two abreast, the line maybe a mile
long. They were union men and miners and lots of them had to be the same ones
who've been up in the hills hiding out and attacking when they could. But nobody
wore a bandanna today, and as many as owned one wore a suit. Like lots of
fellows, I joined the march at the tail, and I felt right about it because Mr. Tikas
had been square with me and tried to keep me safe, and I'd seen enough of him
to understand why so many wanted to pay their last respects.

I FINALLY REACHED Ben Lindsey by telephone at his home on
Saturday evening. In the walk back to the center of Trinidad from
the cemetery, I had spoken with a fellow who introduced himself as
Doyle and who said he was from the United Mine Workers' office
in Denver. The man, whose accent reminded me of the way my

mother shaped her words, had contended that everyone in the city except the stinking bourgeoisie was up in arms about what had happened at Ludlow, and although *bourgeoisie* was a word that was new to me, the way in which Doyle had spit it out seemed to offer a sort of definition.

You bet I've heard of Judge Ben Lindsey, Doyle said when I broached his name. Bloody fine chap he is, by all accounts. And Doyle had insisted that the telephone at the union's local on Main Street was mine to use if I needed to get news to Lindsey.

The first thing the judge wanted to know as an operator connected us was whether I was all right. Had I been caught in any of the fighting?

I got cuffed up a bit is all, I told him, my voice awkwardly loud in an attempt to be heard across the 180 miles. I had a fit, as it happened, and funny thing is, it may have saved me from worse.

I had no intention to put you so directly in harm's way, the judge told me apologetically. I do hope you're all right, Son.

Fine, Sir. But I'm afraid I've spent most of your money on a bed these last nights.

Good for you. Do you have enough left for a ticket home? I want you to come back tomorrow.

Yes, Sir. That'll be fine.

Should I telephone your mother? Does she know you're there?

No. Mostly I don't tell her much about my regular business. She says it's best that way because she worries.

Do you know where I live? I want you to come to my house as soon as you get to town tomorrow.

I don't know the number, but I know the house. On Ogden

Street. I've written a lot down that I've seen, and I meant for you to read it.

Good.

Some of it's been pretty bad, I told the judge, whose voice had gone faint, before I handed the telephone's earpiece to Doyle and thanked him for the bother.

Bother? Not for a second, son, said Doyle, applying a hand to my shoulder. Solidarity is all it is. Then Doyle suggested that a good ale would help us slake the bitter taste of the day, and I joined him for the short walk to a dour saloon where he already was well known. Our two beers soon were four, and then four more, and the place grew boisterous with workingmen who toasted with besotted sorrow the memory of the martyred Louis Tikas. I was drunk for the first time since I'd boarded a train in Denver nearly a week before, and the languid haze of alcohol was a pleasure I welcomed that evening. Its daze felt light and buoyant and supportive, and I reveled as well in Doyle's long and boozy soliloquies, stories of remembered fights and labor struggles still to come and some fellow named Marx whom I supposed Doyle had apprenticed with back in Belfast.

As we stood shoulder to shoulder in the establishment's foul pissoir, Doyle said that the unlucky lads who knew just who them murdering soldiers was would be the next to die, and his remark still troubled me as I finally said goodnight then walked for a while through the steep and now-silent streets of Trinidad, the dark sky dripping rain again. I had said nothing to Doyle about the fact that I was with Louis Tikas in his last hours, and now, for the first time since the slaughter, I reckoned that maybe this was information I didn't dare share with anyone. The undertaker could confirm that I had known the locations of the bodies, yet the man hadn't pressed me for stories of that bloody day. But would the judge appreciate the danger—and horde my secret—once I relayed the terrible particulars to him?

I sat down on the wooden steps that led to a butcher shop. I was sheltered from the rain as I leaned against its door, and in the light cast by an overhead bulb, I began to reread in my ledger what I'd written about the events I observed at Ludlow—about the men in the militia as well the man the fellows in the saloon now called a martyr. I had half a mind to throw my book in the river as I walked the streets that led to the boarding house—that would be the slick thing for a fellow to do, goddamnit—yet I tucked the ledger inside my overcoat instead.

ON A TRAIN bound to Denver on Sunday morning, I wrote these words over the whorled design on the frontispiece of my ledger: *Everything set down in here is the writing of Thomas L. Dumont, Address Uncertain, Denver, Colorado, and is the truth as he saw the things he saw.*

JUDGE BEN LINDSEY stood inside the great hall at Union Station and called out my name as I walked in from the platform. The cold rain had come to the city by now and the judge wore a wool coat and a fedora that hid his balding head. The Colorado & Southern train had arrived on schedule, yet I was surprised—and immediately uneasy—to discover that the judge had come to meet me.

I was heading straight to your house, I assured him as the judge extended his hand.

I know you were, but there's a change of plans, and it was a good guess that this was the train you'd catch. Let me look at you.

Some poor fellow left this coat at the depot there in all the commotion, I offered too self-consciously, my disquiet mounting as I quickly manufactured an explanation the judge hadn't requested. I felt bad for him and for the taking of the coat, but I figured he wouldn't be back for it, and with all the rain . . .

Fine coat. I can see that my twenty dollars didn't buy it. And I'm glad to see for myself that you're all right. A rally's been called at the capitol for four o'clock, even with this weather. And a friend of mine is due here shortly from Washington. I realized I could meet you both, then we'll go over and lend our voices.

Fine, I said, allayed that the judge seemed unconcerned about the coat.

At the dining room in the Oxford Hotel a block away, Lindsey ordered tea and toast; I ate pot-roast when the judge pressed me to have a meal, and for most of an hour I described the details of my consequential journey—the days and nights in Ludlow, the grim return trip in the company of the undertaker, the aftermath in raucous Trinidad, the woeful funerals, even the rather more prosaic train rides with the snow-clad Front Range of the Rockies out the window, the two mothering peaks of *Huajatolla* towering above the trouble, the brooding and weeping skies.

It grieves me—sickens me says it better—to think that this state's guard could act so maliciously, Lindsey said, absently stirring his tea. A friend, fellow attorney—Harold Hornsby—is a guard officer posted down there somewhere, and I can't imagine *him* condoning such stuff.

I attended to my roast and did not dare respond, and in the next moment a waxing fright erased my appetite. No Sir, I said at last, dreading the judge's next question, which was all too easy to anticipate.

Did you get any names? Any of the militiamen there that day?

They mostly just called them Major or Lieutenant, you know. Sometimes Sir.

You'd recognize them though?

One fellow, I believe he keeps a saloon on Larimer. Him I'd seen before. The rest, well, there were lots of them and then it got dark . . .

Well, never mind for now.

On the short walk back to Union Station, and in the minutes in which I sat alone on a polished, high-backed bench while the judge went to meet his friend's incoming train, I wrestled with this newest fix: Hornsby's account of how the tents caught fire would be far different from my own, and it would be plainly at odds with the truth of that awful day and night. Hornsby would contend as well, of course, that he knew nothing about how Mr. Tikas had come to be killed, and Judge Ben Lindsey would have to weigh his friend's report with the word of a ragtail who'd been hauled by the ear to court on numerous occasions, and I rued every moment of my southern journey now. With some urgency, I scanned again my penciled story of Ludlow in angry flame, and no, I hadn't scribbled Hornsby's name there, and at least that was minor comfort for the moment. But I hurriedly tucked the ledger away as the judge returned with a small and older woman on his arm, her cloth-covered case carried in his opposite hand.

Thomas Dumont, let me introduce you to one of America's finest citizens, said the judge, his arms spread wide in a gesture meant to embrace both her and me. This is Mrs. Mary Jones.

Mother, she said, correcting Lindsey, offering her hand to me. And I'm just a scrappy old woman who's been on a train too long. I'm pleased to make your acquaintance, Sonny.

Pleased to meet you, Ma'am.

The judge tells me you were at Ludlow in the middle of that terrible business.

Yes, Ma'am.

She shook her head. I know something about the loss of children, and I know, too, that those thugs will burn in bitter hell one day for what they've done. Tell me how you escaped the torture.

Well, I had a fit, Ma'am, which must have saved me. I turned to the judge as if to ask for elaboration and Mother Jones looked at him as well.

Epilepsy, Lindsey explained. Terrible spells overtake him periodically, and we ought to assume that this time a guardian angel simply made the most of one.

We do have constant blessings. Even in troubled times. I'm very happy you're all right, Sonny, but I hope those vermin don't have you marked for more of the same.

We'll take good care of him, Lindsey assured her. But at the moment, we'd better be off to the capitol if we're going to get you there in time to speak.

Judge Ben Lindsey's black Model T Ford was just the sort of car I might have guessed he would own—entirely practical and something less than showy—and I was quick to offer to pull the choke and crank the engine to get us underway. The judge's route to the capitol included Curtis Street, the million electric lights that adorned its blocks of cinemas and burlesques ablaze on that wet and gloomy afternoon, and I was pleased when the dazzling sight caught the famous woman's eye. My land, she said, it's like it's Christmastime. But when we neared the gold-domed capitol that crowned the low hill east of Broadway, the spectacle simply was one of people—thousands of them, bundled against the weather, broad umbrellas capping groups of two and three, the lawns that swept up to its steps and porticos obscured by their enormous numbers.

Would you look at this?, said Lindsey. I can't guess how many have come out to give our dear governor grief.

I'd like to box the bugger's lights out, Mother said with a high-pitched laugh. But I'm on my good behavior today.

It took some minutes to find a place to park the motorcar, and a brass band was playing "La Marseillaise" as the three of us wound through the crowd that flanked the capitol on two sides. When we reached the top of the steps where a wooden dais had been constructed, the judge explained to Mother Jones that the man exhorting the crowd at the moment was his friend George Creel, the burly fellow an editorial writer for the *Rocky Mountain News* and likely the only man in Denver whose progressive zeal and constant indignation eclipsed his own. Good George is cut from your kind of cloth, Lindsey confided to her with a smile.

The martyrs of Ludlow did not die in vain, we and the many

thousands now heard the journalist shout.

They have written with their blood upon the wall of the world. The Rockefellers who profess Christ in public and crucify Him in private have been unmasked, and never again will the patter of prayers be permitted to excuse Judas's greed. The current system must be smashed to bits! That is the challenge Ludlow puts to those who sit in the seat of the mighty, wrapping the flag about their profits, putting their assassins in militia uniforms, buying law and legislators, and crying out against class prejudice even while they draw class lines with the point of a bayonet!

Next, Creel's invective turned to the traitor Elias Ammons, the scandalous Colorado governor and corrupt rancher whose sympathies for cattle far outweighed his compassion for the downtrodden people of his state, as far as Creel was concerned, and as the crowd roared its concurrence with that assessment, Lindsey was able to catch Creel's eye and show him that at last the much-anticipated final speaker had arrived. Creel's segue into his introduction of Mother Jones was quick and effortless, but his praise for her was the effusive and florid sort she hated, so overdone finally that she couldn't bear to let him finish, marching into view as Creel still spoke and throwing her prim hat into the ocean of clustered faces, raising her arms like a prizefighter claiming a violent victory. Two union men gleefully waved the Stars and Stripes and the Union battle flag on either side of her, and the crowd now clamored its welcome.

Here I am again, boys, she shouted as loud as her small voice let her when the din slowly settled.

I'm just back from Washington, and the news I have for you is that you aren't licked by a whole lot. Just keep your heads level and don't do anything to disgrace the state. The state is all right. Like Mr. Creel told you, it's just a few fools at the head of things that are bad. Don't commit any depredations. Washington is aroused, I can promise you that, and there is help coming. We'll make some laws to put the Colorado Fuel and Iron Company out of business. And we'll send Mr. Rockefeller back to Sunday school, but this time he'll be the pupil instead of the teacher. We'll teach him something of the Golden Rule, and put an end to his filthy, murdering ways. I found this governor thing of yours in Washington trying to save some trees when I got there. I told him, God Almighty, save the people and let the trees alone! Back home you have murder of women and children and here you are praying for the trees. But we'll win out. They'll never crush a principle, and they never will stop me as long as I have breath. Now then, you boys all go home. Mind me now and keep cool. Stay out of the saloons, save your money, and when I'm ready I'll call for you. Be patient, boys, be strong and smart. But by God, boys, remember Ludlow!

I HEARD JUDGE Ben Lindsey say that it must have been the shortest speech she ever gave. But you can't imagine how the crowd loved hearing what Mother had to say. It seems odd to call her that, but that's how she told me to address her. I reckon she's nearly the most famous person I've ever met. More than Senator Guggenheim, who I knew back when I still lived at home, but less, I'd say than

Bill Cody, who everybody in my family's known forever.

They sang the same union song I heard at Ludlow at the close, then after the rally was over Mother Jones and the judge drove off to his house, where Mrs. Lindsey had supper ready, he said, and where she was their guest for the night. He didn't invite me along and I was glad of it because the truth is that I'd had enough for the time being of strikes and politics and killings. What I was looking for was just my regular life again for a little while, and I sure wanted to flush the worry about Hornsby and all I saw out of my thinking if I could. But before I said so long to them, the judge was stern about telling me to stay in touch with him. He said he wanted to read my ledger book, and I said sure, though I didn't really mean it anymore.

What I did then was walk back to the St. Elmo Hotel since the rain had let up and I always feel like walking when there's something to think about. Because it was a Sunday evening, I figured Belle Kelly might not be busy working, so I called up to her room from downstairs. She asked me where in the world I'd been hiding myself and I said something about a job on a farm in Littleton. I told her I was mighty in the mood to go over to Chin Lee's to hit the pipe for a little while, and she said my timing was just so because it sounded fine to her.

I waited for her downstairs and then we walked on up Market to the alley behind Tessa Randolph's rooming house, where Belle worked when I first met her. It was Belle who first took me to Mr. Chin's, but nowadays he knows both of us real well, and he took us to a tiny room with two cots that we could have to ourselves, and then Chin's son with the long jet braid that Belle admires brought us a full pipe and I let go of everything for the first time since the judge sent me south. I always like a smoke after I've had a fit. It almost always helps with the headache, and it puts me into a fog I feel good inside, and the next morning that wooziness from the fit is long gone. But then, I also like the pipe most any time, though my finances don't support it too often. Belle is more regular than me, I know, partly because she has such steady employment, but also because entertaining men isn't easy work, and sometimes she just needs the hazy dreams of a different life.

I always called her Mrs. Kelly until after the first time she took me up to her room and told me I know her too well to call her anything but Belle. She comes from Clare, same as my mother's family, though I don't think she's quite as old as my mother is. She's as fine to me, at any rate, as my mother, and I sure did want to tell her about everything from the last few days, and I know she could tell I was stewing over something, but I was afraid to talk to anyone, and then we both sort of drifted into quiet.

You feel like you're fairly floating when you finally climb the stairs out of Mr. Chin's—or like you're floating through the sky, although I'm afraid my fits are going to keep me from flying and ever knowing that for sure. Belle and I made our way back to the St. Elmo after a while. She asked me if I had a room for the night, then said I'd better come up when I told her no. I think she was glad enough to have me for the company, and I don't suppose she thought I'd wake her wanting favors since I'd been sucking bamboo. She instructed me to take a bath in her big tub and I was glad to obey. She lounged on her bed and sang me a song in the old Irish language, and she called me her darlin' boy. And she told me that on that night, at least, the world didn't own any trouble.

Author's Note

FRENCH AVIATOR LOUIS Paulhan did indeed make the first flight in a powered airplane in Denver in February 1910. There is no record that William F. "Buffalo Bill" Cody was in attendance on any of the three days Paulhan flew in Denver, but he almost certainly would have wanted to be. His touring show, "Buffalo Bill's Wild West," played to sold-out crowds for many years throughout the United States and Europe. Without doubt, he was the most renowned resident of Denver in all the world during that time.

Judge Ben Lindsey, a writer and social reformer as well as a jurist, served for twenty-eight years on Denver's Juvenile Court bench before he was ousted from his service to the city's poor and indigent children. Margaret Brown, posthumously remembered as "The Unsinkable Molly Brown," was a wealthy and well-liked Denver socialite, philanthropist, and social activist who survived the 1912 sinking of the *Titanic*. Ira "Bumps" Humphreys and his brother Albert E. Humphreys, Jr. were the very well-to-do sons of "The King of the Wildcatters," who discovered oil in Wyoming,

Oklahoma, and Texas before he moved his family to Denver in 1898. The two brothers were fascinated with airplanes and opened Denver's first commercial airport in 1918 at 26th Avenue and Oneida Street in the Park Hill neighborhood ten years prior to the establishment at that location of the Denver Municipal Airport, which eventually became Stapleton International Airport.

Denver's Chinatown was commonly called "Hop Alley" because it was home to numerous opium parlors, which were frequented by people of many ethnicities before and after the turn of the twentieth century. The anti-seizure medication phenobarbital was first marketed in 1912 by the German drug company Bayer under the brand-name Luminal. Initially thought to be efficacious only as a sedative, it became the first drug in the world capable of successfully preventing certain types of epileptic seizures.

Twenty-one striking miners, wives, and children were killed by Colorado National Guardsmen on April 20, 1914, in what became known as the Ludlow Massacre, one of the deadliest labor incidents in U.S. history. Striking miner Louis Tikas, who led the strikers and who was among those murdered, was a Greek immigrant whose many-blocks-long funeral cortège, comprised of literally thousands of striking coal miners and union men, filled the streets of Trinidad, Colorado seven days following the massacre. The United Mine Workers of America finally ran out of money and ended the coal-miners' strike on December 10, 1914. The strikers' demands for better pay and safer working conditions were not met, the union was crushed, and most striking miners were replaced.

George Creel was a passionate social reformer who wrote editorials for the *Denver Post* and, later, the *Rocky Mountain News* before he was appointed Denver police commissioner, a position from which he worked ardently to destroy the city's notorious red-light district. Mary "Mother" Jones was first a schoolteacher and dressmaker, born in Ireland, before she became the most renowned union organizer, community organizer, and activist in American history. She helped coordinate many major strikes and co-founded the Industrial Workers of the World. Mother Jones spoke to an enormous crowd gathered on the steps of the Colorado state capitol in Denver a few days following the Ludlow murders.

A decade following the Ludlow Massacre, Dr. Galen Locke—whose outlandish explanation of the cause of Tommy's epilepsy is responsible for Tommy leaving home—became Grand Dragon of the Ku Klux Klan in Colorado. Under his control, the Colorado Klan gained 40,000 members. In 1924, however, national Klan Imperial Wizard Hiram Evans forced Locke to step down and Locke ultimately spent time in jail for tax evasion.

Other characters like Dr. Galen Locke, Pat Hamrock, Harold Hornsby, and Ed Doyle are closely modeled on their historical namesakes. Isabel Kelly, Tessa Randolph, Avi Sokolow, and Tommy Dumont and his family are entirely fictional. The author imagines that Tommy never was able to realize his dream of becoming an aviator, but that his seizures were eventually well-controlled with medication, and he spent many years as a reporter and columnist for Denver's *Rocky Mountain News*. Perhaps Tommy wrote his memoir of his early dream of flying, his life on the streets and alleys of Denver, and his experiences of the Ludlow Massacre in 1964, on the fiftieth anniversary of the murders, when Tommy would have been sixty-seven.

About the Author

RUSSELL MARTIN'S NONFICTION book *Beethoven's Hair*, a United States bestseller and a *Washington Post* Book of the Year, has been published in twenty-one translated editions and is the subject of a Gemini-award-winning film of the same name. His highly acclaimed book *Picasso's War* has been published in seven international editions; *Out of Silence* was named by *The Bloomsbury Review* as one of the fifteen best books of its first fifteen years of publication, and *A Story That Stands Like a Dam: Glen Canyon and the Struggle for the Soul of the West* won the Caroline Bancroft History Prize.

He directed, produced, and wrote the documentary film *Beautiful Faces*, which won the Silver Palm Award of the Mexico International Film Festival. He produced and co-wrote the Monette Horwitz Prize-winning documentary film *T wo Spirits*, and is an award-winning, internationally published author of two critically acclaimed novels, *The Sorrow of Archaeology* and *Beautiful Islands*, as well as many nonfiction books. He has written for *Time*, the *New York Times*, *New York Times Magazine*, and National Public Radio. His books and screenplays have been optioned by Robert Redford's Wildwood Enterprises, actor Dennis Haysbert, the Denver Center Theatre Company, and New World Television, and he is a veteran script doctor and consultant. He taught an annual creative nonfiction course at Colorado College for two decades and has served on the faculties of numerous writing conferences.

www.ingramcontent.com/pod-product-compliance
Lightning Source LLC
Chambersburg PA
CBHW051145020726
47501CB00005B/1687